"Running away, Keira?"

"I'm not playing power games, Mr. Cassidy. And no means no in my language."

"'No' is not what your body is saying to me," Eden said softly.

"I told you before, I don't sleep around. I never have."

"I don't recall implying that you did," Eden cut in concisely.

"And I don't intend to start with you," Keira continued smoothly. "Don't call me, I'll call you. Oh, and I wouldn't hold my breath waiting for the phone to ring, if I were you."

LYNSEY STEVENS was born in Brisbane, Queensland, and before beginning to write she was a librarian. It was in secondary school that she decided she wanted to be a writer. "Writers, I imagined," Lynsey explains, "lived such exciting lives—traveling to exotic places, making lots of money and not having to work. I have traveled. However, the tax man loves me dearly, and no one told me about typist's backache and frustrating lost words!" When she's not writing she enjoys reading and cross-stitching and she's interested in genealogy.

Lynsey Stevens writes intense, deeply emotional romances with vibrant, believable characters. She loves to write snappy dialogue, and we think you'll agree that the sparks fly between Eden and Keira in *A Physical Affair*.

A Physical Affair

LYNSEY STEVENS

THE MILLIONAIRES

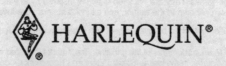

HARLEQUIN®

TORONTO • NEW YORK • LONDON
AMSTERDAM • PARIS • SYDNEY • HAMBURG
STOCKHOLM • ATHENS • TOKYO • MILAN • MADRID
PRAGUE • WARSAW • BUDAPEST • AUCKLAND

ISBN 0-373-80520-9

A PHYSICAL AFFAIR

First North American Publication 2002.

This edition published by arrangement with Harlequin Books S.A.

® and TM are trademarks of the publisher. Trademarks indicated with
® are registered in the United States Patent and Trademark Office, the
Canadian Trade Marks Office and in other countries.

Visit us at www.eHarlequin.com

Printed in U.S.A.

CHAPTER ONE

KEIRA gazed up at the larger-than-life-sized portrait that was so skilfully lit. Eden Cassidy.

Just two short days ago he had merely been the celebrated chief of Cassidy-Ford Publishing Corporation, the media conglomerate that owned the magazine where Keira worked as an assistant editor. Technically he was her boss but she'd never actually met the man whose name and face were known worldwide.

Oh, she'd seen him from a distance at a meeting once and she had to admit he was nothing if not a dynamic speaker. And, to add even more colour, the head of Cassidy-Ford Publishing was also renowned as a man who spoke his mind, who definitely didn't suffer fools gladly. His sparse, very short and to-the-point memos, bearing his strong, forceful signature, attested to that fact.

And then he was regularly interviewed by the whole spectrum of the media who had made tracking him down into almost a national sport.

Now Keira stood in the library of the Cassidy mansion north of Sydney gazing at Eden Cassidy's lifelike image and she shivered with anticipation, mixed with a definite trace of uneasiness. For at some time this weekend she would surely have to come face to face with the man himself.

And, in view of that small incident a short time ago, she had grave doubts that she had made the best of impressions.

Not for the first time she admonished herself for allowing herself to be manoeuvred into this ambivalent position.

Had it only been Thursday morning when Daniel Cassidy had come into her office with his ridiculous request? And as usual he'd interrupted her when she had been up to her ears in work.

"Look, Daniel, I'm far too busy to be discussing this with you now. As well you know," Keira had berated him without glancing up from the stack of submissions on her desk.

"All plain excuses, Keira. You could get this magazine out with your hands tied behind your back and your eyes closed." Daniel leant across her desk to blow a puff of breath lightly on her ear. "So, how about it?"

"Daniel!" Keira sat back in her chair, her fingers going involuntarily to her neck where a wisp of fine fair hair had escaped from her chignon. "Don't do that!"

"Ah ha! Now I have your attention." Daniel grinned at her engagingly.

And that he *was* an extremely engaging young man, Keira couldn't deny. Tall. Fair-haired. Blue-eyed. Intelligent. Rich. And, to top it all off, very nice.

"Daniel, please."

"Why won't you come with me?" he asked earnestly.

"Just one minor reason. Because I'm a decade older than you are, that's why."

Daniel gave a scoffing laugh. "How you adults do exaggerate," he mocked. "You are but eight years—"

"Nine," Keira put in, "which is nearly a decade."

"OK," Daniel acquiesced. "You are nine years my senior, which suits me just fine because I'm more than partial to older women."

"At the risk of denting your adolescent ego, I'm not into younger men. Sorry," she added wryly.

"How do you know if you haven't tried one?" He straightened and folded his arms, looking down at her with overstated seriousness. "As a toy boy, I'm renowned, the cream of the crop so to speak."

Keira laughed lightly, wondering what he'd say if she

gave in to the urge to ruffle his stylish fair hair. "I'm sure you are, Daniel. Maybe that's why I wouldn't be able to trust myself with you."

"I can be trusting enough for both of us," he put in quickly, and Keira shook her head.

"Incorrigible, but tenacious." She smiled as she rested her elbows on her desk, her chin in her hands. "Which is why you're going to make a pretty good newspaper man—" she paused and raised her eyebrows "—when you grow up."

"Now that was below the belt." Daniel subsided into the chair behind him and sighed. "Do you really mean that, Keira? The newspaper man bit?"

"Yes, I do. And don't pull the insecure young person performance on me," she said levelly. "You know exactly who and what you are."

At nineteen Daniel Cassidy had more maturity than a lot of thirty-year-olds possessed, Keira knew. Certainly more than Dennis had had. She sighed and pushed her ex-husband out of her mind.

"And for what it's worth," Keira continued, "I find that admirable."

Daniel pursed his lips. "Then why won't you come with me on Saturday? It's only until after lunch on Sunday and I promise you'll have your own room. With a lock. And a chain. Should any lecherous intentions arise," he added with an impertinent twinkle in his eyes.

With no little difficulty Keira controlled the blush that threatened to colour her cheeks. Fair skin had more disadvantages than the fact that it was susceptible to the sun. She had just turned twenty-eight, for heaven's sake. She had married at twenty, been divorced at twenty-five, so one would expect she'd be long past being embarrassed by a teasing innuendo.

Usually she could handle it. But just occasionally the naïve little nobody who'd fallen for a handsome face and the thoughts of babies and a pretty little suburban cottage sprang out to remind her.

"I can't understand why you don't ask one of the hordes of dead gorgeous girls of a socially acceptable age for a nineteen-year-old male. They'd all be more than willing and would rush to spend the weekend at the Cassidy mansion," Keira remarked, and added quickly in defiance of her old self, "If you did there could be an added bonus and, dare I voice the indelicate, you could get lucky."

Daniel feigned shock. "Bawdiness doesn't become you, my dear." He grimaced and shook his head. "I hate casual sex. I told you. I want a meaningful relationship."

"Then spend some time getting to know someone your own age."

Daniel said something unprintable under his breath. "They're mostly so…so boring. Older women are—" He shrugged. "I just like older women. But apart from that, you have to come, Keira," he said softly. "I've told the family you will."

"The family?" Keira questioned absently, her mind half on the work on her desk.

"Well, my uncle."

Keira's backbone straightened, her full attention now on Daniel, and she gazed at him in surprise. "You what?"

"I just…" He ran his hand through his hair. "Oh, hell, Keira. He forced my hand. I was provoked."

"Provoked? You actually told him I was…? You mentioned me by name?"

"Well, Eden said with his usual sarcasm, 'And this is a special occasion, Daniel, so if you must bring one of your giggling air-heads, make sure she knows her fork from her spoon'," Daniel mimicked. "I lost my cool, Keira."

Keira could understand that. She also wondered if Daniel knew just how like his well-known uncle he sounded. Eden Cassidy was an older, usually unsmiling, dark-haired version of Daniel, his late older brother's son.

"Well, he doesn't know me," Keira frowned, "so you can simply tell him you've made other arrangements."

"He knows you by name," Daniel remarked and grimaced. "Keira Strong and *Chloe* magazine are mentioned conversationally in tandem. Everyone knows you virtually run things here and that old Dingbat Di is just an editor in name only."

"Daniel, I won't have you—"

"All right," he broke in, "you don't want to talk about that either. But Eden does know you work here. And that's gospel."

"He probably won't even remember. I'm just small fry," she murmured almost to herself, and then looked back at Daniel. "You've said yourself your uncle lives to work. And what with everything else he must surely have on his mind, well, this magazine is just a tiny cog in the wheels of Cassidy-Ford Publishing."

"Huh!" Daniel sat forward. "No go, Keira. The man has a mind like a computer. He never, but never, forgets a thing. He knew you were with this magazine and he'll be expecting you in person."

"Daniel, for heaven's sake!"

"Can't you look on it as a business meeting?" Daniel suggested.

"A business meeting? Your grandfather's eightieth birthday celebration?"

"Well—" Daniel began.

"Since your grandfather is Sir Samuel Ford, co-founder of this illustrious and gigantic media conglomerate, I hardly think we can write off the weekend at the family mansion as a business meeting, do you?"

Daniel shrugged. "On past performances there'll be thousands of people there, all vying for top attention. We won't even be noticed."

Keira gave a sharp laugh of disbelief. "Oh, no? The only grandson of Sir Samuel Ford will be pushed right out of the limelight." Keira shook her head. "Really, Daniel! If you were the young brother I think of you as I'd—well, I'd do something very physical to you."

"Promises, promises." He held up his hand at Keira's expression. "I'm sorry. But you know I hate going out to the family seat for the weekend. I thought if you were going to be there it would be bearable. I mean, Eden always gets on my back about going to university, old Sam quizzes me about girls." He sighed loudly. "He wants a great-grandson, would you believe? No one pressures Eden about producing an heir to take over the family fortune. I tell you, Keira, it's a hell of a life."

She had to smile, if reluctantly, and Daniel pulled his chair closer, reaching across her desk to clasp her hand. "But apart from that, don't you see, Keira? That's why I like you. The money—it doesn't rate with you. I know you like me for myself. You aren't after the cash and the name and everything. Most girls are, you know."

He could be right about that, Keira acknowledged, and then removed her hand from his. "Very clever, Daniel. But the poor little rich boy act won't wash either. However, don't despair, you nearly had me there."

He laughed softly. "I do really like you, you know. How could I not? You're attractive, intelligent, funny. And I can talk to you. Can't you do me this one small favour?"

"No, Daniel."

"Then you'll be wasting Eden's spot of investigation."

Keira paused and glanced up from the article in front of her. It's another ploy. Ignore it, Keira, she told herself, knowing full well she wouldn't and that she'd regret asking. "Investigation? What investigation?"

"Well, you don't think Eden Cassidy would take any girl I'd date, one I'd bring to old Sam's party no less, at face value, do you?"

"Absolute rubbish." She frowned. Was this another of Daniel's tactics? "You said yourself he knew all about me."

"Not all about you. Knew of you. Now you've been checked out. Hasn't there been someone around the office this past week just asking a few unassuming questions, almost invisibly watching the comings and goings?"

"Daniel, that's ridiculous." Keira caught her breath. There was someone. A nondescript man of indiscernible age. But he'd said he was part of the time and motion... He'd had credentials. It had started rumours of revamping the magazine, although Keira personally had disregarded the idea.

She looked levelly at Daniel. "Are you making this up?"

He shook his head and Keira stood up to pace behind her desk.

What a rotten thing to do. Eden Cassidy wouldn't have the gall to investigate her for so paltry a reason. Not face to face. Well, face to face if only through one of his minions, so to speak. He could have simply checked her file in personnel without going to such elaborate lengths. "He wouldn't dare," she breathed.

"Wouldn't he?"

The sound of Daniel's voice brought her back from her cloud of anger and she looked at him through narrowed eyes. "Is this on the level?"

He nodded solemnly.

"Good grief! Just because he's the king pin it doesn't mean he can..." She paused, seeking the right words. "It's an invasion of privacy, that's what it is. He must think he owns us. Do you know, I should front up to him and tell him to his face what a manipulative..." Keira closed her mouth and bit back the rest of the unflattering adjectives she was thinking in conjunction with Eden Cassidy.

"He sure has a nerve, doesn't he? Thinking he can dictate someone's after-hours life." Daniel stood up and rubbed his hands together. "And this weekend would be the greatest opportunity for you to show him he has no claim on you after you've put in your forty hours." He raised his eyebrows. "What say I pick you up about eight-thirty on Saturday morning?"

And what a fantastic display of Cassidy manipulation, Keira told herself for the umpteenth time as she'd snapped shut the catch on her overnight case this morning and set it by the front door. The dynamic Eden Cassidy would have been proud of his only nephew.

"Manoeuvred into going away for the weekend with a boy still in his teens," she muttered aloud as she gazed down at her sleeping cat. "To a party for a self-made billionaire which is to take place in the family mansion. And said family mansion just so happens to be a showpiece that has held its own in the hierarchy of lifestyles of the rich and famous. What do you think about that, Roger?"

The dark ball of fur remained stationary, apart from one very slight flick of the end of his tail.

Keira tried to rub the tension from her brow. At this rate she'd be starting out with a headache. "Sounds as if a great time will be had by all, doesn't it, Roger? Well, you haven't heard the half of it. That's just the boring old cake. The icing is having to meet the ruthless, egotistical, despotic Eden Cassidy."

The tail tip again flicked unimpressedly.

"Big help you are." Keira sighed as she walked down the hallway of her bungalow, for once not seeing its attractive appointments.

The cottage had been smaller when her only aunt had owned it, and it had been Keira's haven since her divorce. Aunt Aggie had left it to her and, with the money she'd received when the small magazine she'd been a partner in had been bought out by Cassidy-Ford Publishing, she'd extended and modernised the well situated house.

As you walked in the door the two bedrooms, one on either side, led off the hall, followed by a bathroom, a small study and the living-room on the left and the pantry, the kitchen and dining-room on the right. Out back Keira had added a wooden veranda, with a full-sized spa pool on the right, all screened for privacy by natural pine woodwork. The deck overlooked the tangle of trees and natural scrub behind the house.

But this morning she'd been too wrapped up in her tortured thoughts to give the house a glance. And she'd barely heard the knock on her door.

"Your carriage awaits, *madame*." Daniel stepped inside the open door as Keira walked towards him. He wore faded jeans and a T-shirt that, although equally well-worn, reeked of some obviously expensive designer label. "I like your place," he added as he looked past her.

"Yes, well, let's go, Daniel. Before I decide to listen to my instincts and change my mind about going." Keira turned to pick up her suitcase but he gallantly took it from her.

"Now don't tell me you don't like sports cars," Daniel exclaimed as Keira hung back when he swung open the door of the red Mazda MX5.

"The car's fine. I'm just a little worried about the sport who's going to get behind the wheel."

Daniel grinned and then sobered. "No worries there, Keira. I can assure you I'm a careful and considerate driver."

And as they pulled up in the gateway of Daniel's home over an hour later and waited for the electronically controlled gates to swing open, Keira could only admire Daniel's driving skill. She glanced sideways at him. He was really an extraordinarily mature young man for his age. His family should be proud of him.

So why would his uncle think he'd be bringing—what had Daniel said?—a giggling air-head to his grandfather's party? Perhaps Eden Cassidy hadn't taken the time to get to know his own nephew, who had been his ward since Daniel was orphaned when he was ten years old. Eden

Cassidy was probably too busy checking up on his staff and making millions on top of his millions.

Sounded fairly typical, she reflected, pushing aside the thought that she was prejudging a situation when she'd only heard one side of it, one biased side at that. From Daniel.

"Here we are. The family shack." Daniel drew up in front of the majestic home.

"Shack, Daniel?" Keira gave a laugh. "By no stretch of the imagination could you call this a shack. You could lose someone in there and not find them for days."

"Too true. And the only good thing about it, as far as I was concerned when I was a kid." Daniel grinned as he lifted their bags out of the boot and handed them to the man who came down the steps to meet them. "This is Mrs Strong, Burton. Perhaps you could put her in the front green room, down the hall from me."

Keira felt herself flush and busied herself slinging the strap of her bag over her shoulder. She could throttle Daniel. What must the man be thinking?

"If you'll come this way, madam." The butler led the way up the steps into the marble-tiled foyer. Moving to his left, he pressed a button for what turned out to be a lift.

Keira raised her eyebrows and Daniel smiled.

"All mod cons, as they say. There are three floors, four counting the attics. If we didn't have the lift we'd spend all our time commuting from one level of the house to the other."

They moved silently upwards and Daniel rolled his eyes at Keira. "Is my uncle home?" he asked the butler's straight back as they stepped into the second floor hallway.

"We're expecting him within the hour." The butler opened a door and motioned Keira to enter. "I hope you'll be comfortable here, Mrs Strong. The intercom is just there by the door. If you require anything, please push this button and it will connect you with the staff."

"Thank you," Keira acknowledged, and when the butler had excused himself she gazed around her in admiration.

"Well? What's the verdict?" Daniel closed the door and leant back against it.

"Need you ask? It's divine." The room was huge, finished in greens and metallic gold. She crossed to the open double doors and stepped out on to her own small balcony.

The grounds of the Cassidy estate swept below her, exquisitely landscaped with trimmed green lawns, clipped hedges, native bushes and colourful flower-filled garden beds. The white curving drive ended at the security gates in the high wall that enclosed the extensive property.

"What a fabulous view. I didn't realise the house was positioned so much higher than the surrounding area." Keira half turned as Daniel joined her, casually resting his arm about her shoulders.

"Just think, my dear Keira, this could all be yours." Daniel leered at her and twirled an imaginary moustache. "Just say the word."

"Quit while you're ahead, Daniel," Keira admonished him. "Because I still haven't forgiven you for that throwaway line in front of poor Burton. I dread even to surmise what he's thinking."

"Burton wouldn't think of thinking anything. You know, you look beautiful when you put on that schoolmarmy face." And before Keira could move, and she was restricted by the small confines of the balcony, Daniel had planted a quick kiss on her lips.

She stiffened, her hands sliding up to push him away. But it wasn't necessary for he had already drawn back, his eyes alight with amusement.

"Gotcha!" he said teasingly, his hand now resting lightly on her waist.

As kisses went it was just a brotherly peck, but Keira frowned at him. "Look, Daniel—"

He held up his other hand. "Sorry, Keira. The devil made

me do it. I wasn't coming on to you. Honestly. It was just
a thank you for coming.''

Keira shook her head at his boyish grin. ''Once more.
Just once more, Daniel Cassidy, and party or no party, I'm
out of here. And I mean it.''

''Well, if you weren't so irresistibly attractive—'' Daniel
began, only to break off as a car door slammed below them.

They both turned to look over the balcony rail, Daniel's
arm still resting about Keira's waist.

A sleek, indigo-blue Jaguar squatted sedately below, a
dark splash on the white pebbled drive, and Burton was
removing a suitcase from the open boot.

But Keira barely noticed him. Her attention was fixed on
the tall dark-haired man who stood, hand on the open car
door, looking up at them.

Eden Cassidy in the flesh. And he wasn't smiling.

Keira's eyes locked with the sparkling dark brilliance of
his, and even with the distance separating her from him she
saw his lips tighten. His gaze narrowed, went from Keira to
his nephew, and back to Keira. And he quite obviously
wasn't pleased with what he saw.

It was only as Daniel's uncle moved towards the steps
that Keira realised he hadn't been alone in the dark Jaguar
XJS.

The woman who had climbed from the car to join him
was almost as tall as he was, Keira judged. Her straight
tailored skirt and contrasting emerald-green blouse clung to
her willowy figure as though they had been cut to fit her
personally. And they probably had, Keira decided. She had
a matching jacket folded over her arm and she carried a
leather briefcase which she refused to trust to the butler.

Unconsciously Keira was leaning slightly over the balcony as she watched the couple below disappear into the
house. Daniel's voice in her ear brought her to the realisation with a jolt, and her hand went to clasp the balcony rail
for instinctive support.

"That was my uncle," Daniel said unnecessarily, and Keira bit off an angry retort.

She drew a deep breath. "I know. And your little display must have been perfectly timed." She swept past him into the bedroom and swung to face him as he followed her. "How could you, Daniel?"

"How could I what?" he appealed.

"How could I what?" Keira mimicked him mercilessly. "Don't act so innocent. Playact that intimate little scene out there, that's what. How could you embarrass me like that?"

"Playact?" Daniel repeated, all wounded affront. "You think I only kissed you because I saw my uncle coming up the driveway?"

Keira's expression was reply enough.

"It doesn't appear to have occurred to you that I might have kissed you because I wanted to, because you looked so bloody attractive I was overcome by my emotions."

"You're treading on very thin ice, Daniel," Keira enunciated succinctly. "This is not the time to clomp about in hob-nailed boots, believe me."

Daniel's lips quirked a moment before his laughter slipped out. "Hob-nailed boots? Heaven forbid. Far too heavy-handed. Subtlety's my middle name."

"Daniel, if I thought you set this up—"

"I didn't stage it, Keira, I swear," he said earnestly. "Not that I wouldn't have if I'd thought of it."

"Oh, Daniel, I'm absolutely livid with you. Can't you see how it would have looked, how...?" Keira shook her head and put some space between them.

"He probably didn't even notice us anyway," Daniel contended easily, and Keira let out a breath in disbelief. "Trust me, when he's in the car Eden spends most of his time on the phone or with his head stuck in his papers. Megan drives. Didn't you notice Megan was at the wheel?"

"Megan?" Keira queried.

"Mmm. Megan Donnelly. Eden's secretary, for want of

a better word.'' Daniel laughed shortly. ''Or Girl Friday, his right arm, his assistant, whatever you like to call her as long as it has to do with 'indispensable'. And I suspect she sees to more than just driving and ordering stationery.''

Keira flushed slightly at his implication, a small frown shadowing her brow. So what if Eden Cassidy and the cool-looking Megan Donnelly had more than a business relationship? The man couldn't work twenty-four hours a day, could he? Although rumour had it that he did. And apart from anything else, it was hardly her business.

No, Keira thought, it had nothing to do with her what Eden Cassidy did with his time. She forced her speculation from her mind, realising Daniel had expertly turned her attention from their previous altercation.

''Although—'' Daniel held up his hand ''—I have often wondered if Eden's friend, Kyle Ferguson, hasn't lived in hope of Megan's attention all these years. But she's usually with Eden.''

''Look, Daniel. You know I agreed to this weekend, against my better judgement, but as a favour to you, on the understanding that it was purely platonic. I expected you to keep your part of the bargain.''

Daniel shrugged. ''OK. I'm sorry, Keira. I didn't mean to embarrass you.''

Keira sighed, reflecting that Daniel was going to match his acclaimed uncle in the manipulative stakes, if even half of the reports she'd heard about Eden Cassidy were true.

''Let's start from scratch,'' Daniel suggested, and glanced at his wristwatch. ''There's time for a quick game of tennis before lunch. How about it?''

''What about your uncle. Shouldn't you—well, go down and—''

''He knows I'm here,'' Daniel said off-handedly. ''He's probably holed up in his study anyhow.''

''On Saturday? I mean, on Saturday at home?'' Surely the man switched off some time.

"Saturday. Sunday. Here or in the city office. He's at the controls every day." Daniel shrugged. "Even in the middle of the night. The man never seems to sleep. So, did you bring your tennis gear?"

Keira nodded.

"Then I'll meet you down in the library in five minutes," Daniel challenged.

"Make it ten minutes, and where exactly is the library?" Keira asked him resignedly.

"Just step out of the lift, turn left through the foyer into the main hall and it's the first door on the left. It looks out over the front of the house. Ten minutes, all right?" Daniel gave her a grin and left her.

In less than the stipulated time she had walked out of the lift and through into the hall. Her step had faltered as she gazed open-mouthed at the magnificence of the marble floors, the elegance of the decor, the huge curved staircase that rose to the balcony above. The artwork on the walls must be worth a fortune, she mused as she crossed the floor, only just overcoming a reflex urge to tiptoe.

The library door was open and she put a tentative foot inside, feeling just a little as though she'd stepped on to the movie set of a big budget soapie.

The room was also huge, and between the dark wooden bookcases that lined all four walls were hung four large paintings. One, Keira saw, was of Daniel, another two of Daniel's grandfathers, obviously painted when Samuel Ford and William Cassidy were little more than Daniel's age.

But it was the fourth portrait, hanging above the large fireplace which was set into the outside wall, that drew her attention. And here she now stood with Eden Cassidy's likeness gazing down at her with that same cold regard she'd experienced from the balcony a short time before.

Yes, what an auspicious start she'd made to the weekend, Keira reflected, unable to break that compelling regard. Eden Cassidy quite probably had completely the wrong idea about her relationship with his nephew. If he cared, that was. He surely didn't seem to show much interest in Daniel.

"What do you think of it?" Daniel's voice coming from behind her made Keira jump. He wore white shorts and an aqua shirt and carried his tennis racket. "Pretty impressive, isn't he?"

"I was going to say I could see the family resemblance but I don't want to encourage you," she said drily as Daniel crossed the thick patterned carpet to stand beside her.

"I didn't think I needed any encouragement," Daniel quipped. "Did you see the one of me over there? I had to pose for that on my eighteenth birthday. What a drag that was."

"I thought you were more like your uncle," Keira reflected, "but now I see Sir Samuel's portrait I'm not so sure."

"You thought I was like Eden?" Daniel pulled a face and rested his hand on Keira's shoulder. "I'm not a bit like him. I told you he was a computerised robot. He programmes himself every Monday morning for the week, and then off he goes, no distractions allowed to intrude."

"I think you're exaggerating, Daniel. He must be incredibly busy when you consider the extent of Cassidy-Ford's holdings."

"I kid you not, Keira. Eden's a damn robot. He's programmed for work and precious few of life's necessities. Eat. Sleep. Shower." Tucking his tennis racket under his arm, Daniel marked off the points on the fingers of his free hand before returning it to rest on her shoulder. "And allowing for his age he probably even programmes himself for a few minutes' roll in the hay once a month or so. Between overseas phone calls, that is."

Before Keira could remonstrate with Daniel, a sound behind them had them both spinning around to face the open door. Like a couple of children caught with their fingers in the cookie jar, Keira decided later.

Eden Cassidy stood regarding them, his eyelashes shielding the expression in his eyes.

Had he heard Daniel's outrageous words? Of course he had, Keira knew. It was in the cold set of his jaw, the tension in his tall body. And he was, Keira had to acknowledge, even more compellingly attractive in real life.

He moved slightly, his attention centring on his nephew. "There's a call for you, Daniel. Take it in my office." Dark eyes seemed to settle on the spot where Daniel's shoulder touched Keira's, for Daniel had moved instinctively closer to her before his uncle spoke.

Keira felt the tension in the younger man and knew his gaze was warring with his uncle's.

"Who is it?" he asked, his voice, only faintly higher than normal, betraying his discomposure.

Eden glanced pointedly at Keira and then shrugged one broad shoulder. "Does the name Cat mean anything to you?"

Out of the corner of her eye Keira saw a slight flush colour Daniel's cheeks, and he darted a quick look sideways at her before replying, "Oh. Yes. An old friend from school." He turned to Keira then. "Please excuse me for a moment, Keira. I won't be long." Yet still he paused slightly before eventually crossing to the door.

And leaving Keira to face his formidable uncle.

The silence stretched between them until Keira was convinced it was echoing screamingly into the exquisite mouldings of the high ceiling of the library. Her throat had contracted and she craved a soothing glass of water.

Eden Cassidy remained silent.

He was doing it on purpose, Keira told herself, using one of his high-powered tactics on her. Well, he'd picked the wrong victim. She swallowed resolutely and forced her vocal cords to work.

"How do you do, Mr Cassidy? I'm Keira Strong." Her voice sounded a little thin in her ears.

"I know." He inclined his dark head. "I'm pleased to meet you at last."

Like hell he was. Keira's chin rose unconsciously. Well, she could also play this social game.

"Daniel was just showing me the family portraits," she began, indicating the artificially lit paintings on the walls about them.

"Was he?" There was no mistaking the obvious cynicism in his tone and Keira swallowed, determined he wasn't going to disconcert her.

"I was just telling Daniel," she continued as breezily as she could, "that he's very much like his maternal grandfather." She stretched the truth. "Perhaps because they have the same colouring," she finished quickly before her voice gave out on her.

Eden Cassidy made no comment and Keira rushed on into the unsettling silence. "He was telling me on the drive out here that your grandfather, William Cassidy, and Sir Samuel Ford went into partnership, bought a small publishing company and built it into the media giant it is today," Keira recited the well-known story and Eden Cassidy grimaced.

"That they did. And no doubt Daniel filled you in on the more colourful tale of his grandfathers."

Keira shook her head, raising her eyebrows questioningly.

"I'm surprised. Daniel enjoys relating the family legend of Sam Ford and William Cassidy both falling in love with the same girl, Maryann Rogers, and that she eventually chose William. William and Maryann had two sons, Michael and myself, and eventually Sam married someone else and had a daughter, Chloe. Then my brother, Michael, married Chloe, thus producing Daniel. Romantic little story, isn't it?"

Keira smiled. "Sam must have been pleased when Daniel's parents married."

"Almost as ecstatic as he was when Daniel was born."

Eden gazed levelly at Keira before he straightened and took a couple of measured steps into the room.

Keira had to call on all her self-control to maintain her position, to stand fast and not step back from him as she desperately wanted to do. Her senses shrieked, all signals blaring a warning, and she knew an almost overwhelming urge to flee.

"Daniel's the apple of Sam's eye. He has—Sam and I both have—great hopes for Daniel," he remarked without inflection, his steady gaze still impaling her.

His eyes were blue, she saw with surprise, not the black she'd imagined from the height of the balcony, and they held a cold intensity that made her shiver. She moved slightly to disguise the tremor that tingled along her spine as his gaze flicked swiftly over her.

"I'm surprised we haven't met before, Mrs Strong," he said now, his tone belying the casual words, and his change of topic threw Keira more off balance. "You've been working for Cassidy-Ford Publishing for five or six years I believe."

"Five years." Keira felt rather like a student standing before a tyrannical headmaster. It would seem he didn't remember his gigantic company taking over their small publication. "But then *Chloe* magazine, although quite successful in its own right, is but a small facet of the overall corporation," she added quickly, hoping the hands holding her tennis racket weren't revealing her nervousness.

He inclined his head again. "But it's most definitely a success. Becoming more so, according to statistics. Due largely to you, so I'm advised."

Keira shifted uncomfortably again. Who had been his informant? Daniel? His time-and-motion spy? "I'm sure that's an exaggeration. It takes a lot of dedicated people working as a team to produce a magazine."

"Granted. But every team needs a guiding hand at the helm."

Which was the job of the editor. "Dianna—" Keira began, only to falter as he lifted one strong tanned hand in a gesture of negation.

"But I don't want to discuss *Chloe* magazine, its editor or its staff at this point," he stated abruptly. "I want to take advantage of Daniel's absence to talk about something quite different."

Some small part of Keira's stomach lurched apprehensively. What could he possibly…? She drew herself together, tried to quell her anxiety, raising her fine eyebrows in what she hoped was an expression of composed moderate interest.

"Yes. Something quite different," he repeated, and folded his arms across his broad chest.

Keira's eye caught the flash of a gold wristwatch as the cuff of his immaculate white shirt slipped back. His long fingers rested on the biceps of his arm and she knew instinctively that the material of his expensive suit covered hard muscle. The tingle of uneasiness in the pit of her stomach changed focus imperceptibly as a sudden spear of a quite diverse tension began to grow. Suddenly her nerve-endings went on an even more critical and complex alert, her blood beginning to quicken in her veins.

"I want to talk about Daniel," Eden Cassidy said levelly.

"Daniel?" Keira's grey eyes met his in a surge of surprised relief.

What had she been thinking? That he had some personal interest in her work? She was just a little self-absorbed, she chastised herself.

He'd said himself they'd never met. And neither could he be expected to recall a business transaction that had been handled by his lawyers over five years ago. He wouldn't even have known she existed had Daniel not commenced work with *Chloe* magazine. He was simply curious about his nephew's progress at what was his first job within the family company.

Relaxing a little, Keira smiled softly, unaware of the slight shift of Eden Cassidy's gaze. It dropped for split-seconds to her full mouth before his own lips tightened and his cold stare returned to meet her eyes.

"Oh. Of course." Keira let out the small breath she'd been holding. "You'll be pleased to hear Daniel's working well. He fits in marvellously with the other staff members and his work is really excellent. You should be so proud of him. He's quite a remarkable young man for his age."

"I see." His dark brows rose somewhat imperiously. "You sound impressed."

"I am. Daniel has great talent," Keira assured him.

Eden Cassidy's compelling blue eyes narrowed. "I'm sure he has," he agreed drily. "Which leads me to the obvious question. Tell me, Mrs Strong—" he paused, his emphasis on the Mrs "—just what are your intentions towards my nephew?"

CHAPTER TWO

KEIRA felt her jaw slacken as she gazed at the man standing a couple of feet from her. Her intentions? Did he mean...? Surely not.

Her grey eyes took in the studied arrogance of his stance, the coldly cynical expression evident in his eyes, eyes as incredibly blue as the deepest reaches of the Pacific Ocean.

If she was unsure of his meaning then those chilling eyes confirmed her suspicions. He meant exactly what she'd suspected his words implied.

Keira's back straightened instinctively and her chin rose. "My intentions? I'm afraid I don't understand what you mean by that," she said succinctly, and they both knew she was stretching the truth.

"Oh, I think you do, Mrs Strong. What are your intentions towards my nephew? I would have thought that was fairly self-explanatory." He made a slightly irritated movement of one well-shaped hand. "However, I'll try to be a little more explicit."

"Please do," Keira put in levelly and his eyes narrowed.

"What would a married woman, one not in her first bloom of youth, want with a teenage boy scarcely out of the classroom, hmm?" He folded his arms across his chest again and held her gaze.

Keira seethed inside. How dared he? How dared he stand there all holier than thou and make such vulgar insinuations? And what precisely did he expect her to say, allowing for the fact that he was, in all essence, her boss? What she'd like to say to him...

"Apart from the obvious, that is?" he added disparagingly, and hot colour flooded Keira's cheeks.

"Daniel and I," she got out between clenched teeth, and then made herself pause, swallow to regain her control. She had to keep her cool, not allow him the satisfaction of nettling her. "Daniel and I are working acquaintances. No more, no less. Daniel kindly—"

Eden Cassidy bit off a derogatory expletive and Keira vehemently wished Daniel were here at this particular moment so that she could give him the sharp edge of her tongue.

"Daniel asked me to accompany him to his grandfather's party as a favour, in a purely friendly capacity."

"So you're just good friends?" Eden mocked sceptically and Keira's lips thinned.

"We are. Daniel is a very nice, intelligent young man. This is the first time I've seen him outside working hours but I must admit I enjoy his company."

"And you expect me to believe that?" Eden Cassidy's hands went to his hips as he glared his so obvious doubt.

"I'm not a liar, Mr Cassidy," Keira informed him directly. "However, you don't need to take my word for it. Check with your nephew if you want to."

"Oh, I do intend to speak to Daniel, make no mistake about that."

Keira felt a momentary pang for Daniel, having to face his uncle's icy wrath, but then she quelled her sympathy. Daniel Cassidy was, after all, to blame for this embarrassing scene.

"But I also felt the need to discuss the situation with you," Eden Cassidy continued smoothly. "You being older than my nephew, and supposedly more mature."

"For heaven's sake," Keira got out. "I'm not that much older than Daniel."

"Oh, come on now, Mrs Strong. You are a number of years older—'' Eden Cassidy put in, but Keira held up her hand negatingly.

"You make it sound as though I'm old enough to be his mother, which is a physical impossibility, apart from the ludicrousness of the idea.'' Her eyes flashed contemptuously over him. "And I resent your implications.''

"Implications?'' Eden Cassidy's dark brows rose. "I thought I was being reasonably specific, Mrs Strong. Let's call it a table card, shall we? So what is it exactly that you resent?'' A cold smile touched his lips and Keira knew an uncharacteristic and almost overwhelming desire to slap his handsome face.

"I have no designs on your nephew's inheritance or his family associations,'' she bit out through clenched teeth. "And whether or not you choose to believe that is irrelevant to me. As for your other ridiculous insinuation, well, it would be laughable if I didn't find it so insulting.''

"I've offended you. My humble apologies.'' He gave a slight bow, his mocking tone contradicting his placating words. "But surely even you, Mrs Strong, must see how your liaison looks.''

Keira marvelled silently that she remained in the same room as this insufferable man. If this was typical of Eden Cassidy she was beginning to understand Daniel's less than favourable view of his uncle. "Daniel and I do not have a *liaison*, Mr Cassidy. As I told you before, we are simply friends.''

"Friends?'' he repeated with that same heavy disbelief.

"Yes, friends, Mr Cassidy,'' she reiterated. "And although it's hardly any of your business, but allowing for the sordid state of your mind, I don't make a habit of sleeping around with men younger than I am.'' Keira realised he would most probably misinterpret her words and added, "Or older than I am, for that matter. You have a nerve to surmise such a thing when you'd never even met me.''

"Such a passionate speech, Mrs Strong. But we're talking about the real world here. The next thing you'll be telling me is that you're just an old-fashioned girl who is happily faithful to her husband." He raised one dark eyebrow with exaggerated scepticism. "A husband who, by the way, happens to be conveniently conspicuous by his absence."

Keira drew herself together. So her company personnel records weren't complete. The great Eden Cassidy didn't know everything. And he thought she had left her husband at home while she enjoyed a weekend of illicit sex with a teenager. Charming!

"There appears to be a hitch in the Cassidy-Ford Publishing archives. Or perhaps your minions have misreported. It must be so difficult to get good snoops these days." Keira unconsciously tapped her leg with her tennis racket.

"Meaning?" He watched her through narrowed eyes.

"Meaning I'm sorry to have to ruin your little fantasy, Mr Cassidy, but I'm not a bored old bag having a fling. However, you are right about one thing. I did, and still do, believe in the sanctity of marriage, so I suppose in the let-it-all-hang-out circles you move in that does make me prosaically old-fashioned.

"Now, I'm more than a little tired of this pointless and humiliating conversation. When Daniel returns I'd appreciate it if you'd inform him that I've gone on to the tennis court."

Keira took two steps towards the door and stopped, turning slightly to look back at Daniel's uncle. "And just a word of advice which you can take or leave. If I were you I wouldn't try to warn Daniel away from me. He's more than a little—" she paused "—disenchanted, shall we say, with some of your ultimatums already. This may be the one to tip the scales completely against you. I'm sure you wouldn't want to do any more damage to your already shaky relationship with your nephew."

"My relationship with my nephew is scarcely any of your business," Eden Cassidy bit out acidly, and Keira knew she'd struck a raw nerve.

"Ordinarily I'd have agreed with you," she told him evenly. "But when the results of this—" she paused "—this preposterous misconception of yours may rebound on me I feel I should protect myself. So I'd appreciate it if you chose your words carefully if you do decide to discuss this with Daniel, because I have no desire whatsoever to have my life complicated by having your nephew thrust into my arms."

Keira took some pleasure in the silent stillness of Eden Cassidy as her flashing eyes held his cold ones for several eloquent seconds. Then, confident that she had had the last word, Keira walked assuredly out of the library and into the hallway that she surmised led to the back of the house and the tennis courts.

Burton materialised almost immediately and at her query gave her the directions she needed. And as she strode along the path the butler had indicated Keira's small surge of success gave way to returning anger.

What right had that man to put her through such a demeaning interrogation? No wonder Daniel always seemed to be at loggerheads with his uncle.

Pacing up and down, she decided she needed to expend some energy on the court to dispel her pent-up anger and she hoped Daniel wouldn't keep her waiting too long.

The arrogance of that man! How dared he jump to such tacky conclusions? Even to suggest she might be interested in Daniel in a physical way... Apart from the slight on her character, the man obviously didn't know his own nephew very well.

In the few short weeks he had been working on the magazine Keira was sure Daniel had revealed more about himself, about his aspirations, than Eden Cassidy knew after living with his nephew for nine years. Although Daniel had a great deal of charm, hence Keira's presence here this weekend, he was definitely not a womaniser. He did flirt a little but it was always good-natured and not in the least offensive. Any conscientious guardian would know that, wouldn't he?

Keira fumed anew, absently bouncing her tennis racket on the open palm of her hand. Intentions, indeed! It would serve Eden Cassidy right if she played up to Daniel and gave his arrogant uncle something to think about.

She should… Keira sighed and pulled a face. She knew what she should do. Pack her bag and leave, leave this palatial mansion, and leave Daniel to his uncle and his family gathering.

But that would be precisely what the omnipotent Eden Cassidy wanted her to do. And, Eden Cassidy aside, it would surely have a young man in Daniel's frame of mind running heroically after her.

No. She'd just have to stay and brazen out the weekend. Who knew? Perhaps she could show Eden Cassidy how badly he had misjudged her character. And his nephew's.

"Hi! Sorry I took so long," Daniel said, his eyes not quite meeting hers as he joined her. "Old school friend. You know how it is?"

Keira shrugged. "Which end do you want?" she asked him, trying to keep her ill humour out of her voice. She had to put Eden Cassidy's impertinence out of her mind and not brood about it, and now was as good a time as any to begin.

"This end will do. Oh—" Daniel paused and turned back to Keira "—what did you think of my uncle?" he asked with studied casualness, his fingers playing with the strings on his racket.

Keira glanced at him sharply but he was regarding her blandly. "What do you want me to say to that, Daniel?" She was equally off-hand and he shrugged.

"Nothing. I just thought—I mean, you said you'd never

met him before, didn't you? And I just wondered—well, what you thought of him.''

What had she thought of him? Initially, that up close he definitely was as attractive as he'd looked on television, as the magazine and newspaper photos depicted. This reflection suddenly, for some inexplicable reason, caused a warm flush to heat her face, and Keira chastised herself. The good looks had certainly been only skin-deep.

''We only spoke for a few minutes. I can't really say I formed an opinion.'' Keira could scarcely believe she had lied so glibly. But what else could she have said to the man's nephew? she asked herself as she tried to justify her prevarication.

''Did you and Eden...? What did you talk about after I left?'' Daniel finished in a rush.

''As I said, we only spoke for a few minutes.''

''I just thought you might have, you know, talked about something.''

''Let me guess.'' Keira had to smile. ''You thought we might have talked about you.'' If you but knew, Daniel, Keira thought to herself.

Daniel moved his shoulders. ''I just had a feeling he might have attempted to get you on his side, sort of twisted your arm to try to convince me I should go to uni instead of deferring for this year.''

''Rest easy, Daniel. We didn't even mention university.'' Keira could almost wish they had.

''That's strange.'' Daniel eyed her speculatively. ''That he'd miss such an opportunity. He doesn't with me.''

''Why would he discuss it with me? And more to the point, why would he imagine I'd have any influence over you?'' Keira's eyes narrowed on Eden Cassidy's nephew. ''Unless you've misled him in some way.''

''About what?'' he asked innocently.

''About us. You and me. Have you, Daniel?'' Perhaps

that would account for his uncle's absurd misunderstanding of the circumstances.

"No. I swear, Keira. Scouts' honour. All I said was you were partnering me to Sam's birthday bash." Daniel frowned, clearly about to question her further, so she turned and moved towards her end of the court.

"OK, how about we play this game of tennis?" she suggested nonchalantly.

"I'm ready when you are." Daniel laughed and spun his racket. "But I think I should be fair and warn you I'm not going to give you any quarter." He paused before adding, "Just because you're an old broad."

"Old…!" Keira gazed at his teasing grin in amazement before bursting out laughing.

"A spectacularly attractive old broad," he added, his grin broadening, "but an old broad for all that."

"I'll give you old broad, Daniel Cassidy. Just let me give you notification that I won't expect any more consideration than I'll be giving someone who's still wet behind the ears."

Two hours later Daniel knocked on the door of Keira's room.

"Your escort for lunch, my dear." He held out his arm very formally, his laughing eyes running over her recently showered figure now dressed in tailored denims and a pale chambray shirt, its cuffs folded neatly back from her wrists. "All refreshed?"

"I think so." She walked beside him to the lift. "But, much as I hate to admit it, my old broad's bones may ache tomorrow."

They laughed together as they stepped into the elevator.

"Burton has lunch set out on the back patio." Daniel glanced at his wristwatch. "And luckily we're not late. He gets his knickers in a knot when I am."

The lift doors slid open and Daniel led the way along the hallway to the right.

"Where did you learn to play tennis like that anyway?" he asked and Keira grinned.

"I had my first lesson when I was eight and I played competitively until I was, oh, about your age." Her smile faltered. Until she had married Dennis and he'd decided the game wasn't something he could better her at so it was phased out. "I used to do pretty well," she added flatly.

"Pretty well?" Daniel rolled his eyes. "I'm no slouch and you sent me to the cleaners. We'll have to have a rematch."

They had reached the double doors that opened out on to a covered patio which overlooked a beautifully landscaped pool a couple of steps below the level of the house. Green fernery hung from the beams of the transparent fibreglass patio roof and the scent of newly mown lawns drifted on the clear air.

A pristine white cloth covered a table that would comfortably seat half a dozen people, and just outside the open double doors was a side table which held bowls of salads, cold meats and fruit.

Daniel handed Keira a plate and helped her to servings of tender carved chicken breast and thinly sliced ham. She relaxed slightly, knowing she had been dreading having to face Eden Cassidy over the meal, and she was more than a little relieved to find Daniel's uncle conspicuous by his absence. So far.

"Will we be dining on our own?" she asked casually as she added crisp lettuce and celery to her plate.

"Probably. You'll have me all to yourself." He shrugged easily when Keira gave him a warning look. "My grandfather's having a light snack in his room. He's decided to rest before the party, which is pretty sensible of him. And Eden never sits down to lunch, he eats on the run."

Daniel spooned potato salad on to his already overflowing plate.

"Eden can't leave his trusty fax machine," he continued.

"In fact I wouldn't be at all surprised if my uncle and his fax were joined at the hip. It would probably take major surgery to separate them."

"Your suspicions are unfounded, Daniel. There's nary a scar," said a deep voice from the doorway, causing Daniel and Keira to start guiltily. "I trust you have no objections if I join you both for lunch."

Keira glanced sideways at Daniel to see his eyes widen as they took in his uncle's relaxed figure as he leaned casually against the door-jamb, strong arms folded.

Eden Cassidy had changed from his formal suit into a pair of grey tailored trousers and a short-sleeved white knit shirt that fitted his muscular body to perfection.

"*I* know." The younger man recovered quickly from his surprise. "Megan's manning the phones and faxes," he suggested easily, and his uncle's lips quirked as he stepped out on to the patio.

"Not the way you mean, Daniel. Megan has a couple of personal calls to make. She'll join us in a while." Eden crossed to the side table and began helping himself to some food.

Before Daniel roused himself to seat her Keira moved on slightly unsteady legs to sit down at the table.

In a formal suit Eden Cassidy's attraction had had a rather remote quality about it. But dressed as he was now, his tanned skin accentuated by the white of his shirt, well, Keira had to acknowledge she wasn't unmoved by his compelling magnetism. He was as charismatic as he was reported to be.

A tiny *frisson* of sensation spiralled in the pit of her stomach and she swallowed to clear her suddenly dry throat. It had been years since a man, any man, had provoked just such a physical response in her, and she knew a shiver of startled trepidation. That it had to be this particular man who was responsible for her unexpected libidinous awareness had her heartbeats fluctuating as much with fear as that more undesirable emotion.

Daniel rushed to take the seat beside her and his uncle calmly slid on to the chair directly opposite her. Keira fancied she could feel the heat emanating from his body where their knees almost touched, and she rather doubted she'd be able to swallow any of the delicious food on her plate.

Her heartbeats continued to behave in a very erratic fashion and she couldn't bring herself to meet what she knew would be coldly cynical blue eyes.

Resolutely she lifted a forkful of food to her mouth and it might have been ashes for all she tasted it. Her wayward senses seemed otherwise engaged. On Eden Cassidy.

Of their own accord her eyes slid from her plate to the white shirt moulding his midriff, moved to his muscular upper arms where the band of his shirt met smooth tanned skin.

Well-developed muscles and a tan. So he didn't spend all his time running his empire, as his nephew had insisted he did.

Keira's eyes rose to the dark V exposed by the open collar of his shirt and her nerve endings began tingling anew. How would it feel to move her lips over that smooth, inviting skin that stretched tautly across his throat, his chest?

Her fork paused on its way to her mouth and she hastily returned the untouched food to her plate. It would have been a mistake to put the food into her mouth. There was no way she could have swallowed anything just at that moment. Her throat had closed on the thunder of her heartbeats in her chest as they rose to all but choke her.

What could she be thinking about? Just a short time ago he had accused her of having an affair with his nephew and yet here she was, sizing up his attractions. And finding them almost irresistibly appealing.

Was she mad? She was completely shocked at her behaviour, behaviour that was so out of character for her. Men had held no interest for her and hadn't since Dennis's perfidiousness had opened her eyes to the fact that knights on white chargers weren't necessarily as princely as they seemed.

This wasn't the time to forget she'd made her choices years ago. All her energies were going into her career. And if, as she had been suspecting of late, she lacked the final drive to push her to the very top, then her achievements to date weren't to be sneezed at. If life went on as it was now she'd be content.

And the very last thing she needed at the moment was a man to complicate things.

She shot another quick glance from beneath her lashes at Eden Cassidy. Especially a man as dangerous as he so obviously was. He had that blatant masculine magnetism that drew a woman's attention, made her wonder impetuously what it would be like to tame such an animal, yet at the same time had her quivering with a heady apprehension at the peril involved in such an adventure.

Keira barely suppressed a self-derogatory laugh. She was getting fanciful in her old age. And foolish. Any woman who deluded herself into thinking she could bring this man to heel was simply asking for trouble of the capital letters variety.

"Did you enjoy your game of tennis?" Eden Cassidy's deep voice broke in on Keira's masochistic reflections and she blinked as she slowly brought her attention back to his words rather than the sound of his so seductive voice.

"Tennis?" she queried absently, and felt Daniel look at her sharply.

"She should have," he put in quickly, and grimaced. "I would have enjoyed it more if I'd won."

His uncle raised one dark brow in Keira's direction. "So you outplayed my nephew, Mrs Strong?" he remarked blandly enough, but the expression in his eyes embroidered his innocent observation.

"Outplayed me? More like slaughtered me." Daniel

grinned good-naturedly. "And the worst part about it is, I think she took it easy with me."

"I assure you, Daniel, I didn't," Keira told him sincerely. "You were a very worthy opponent."

"Perhaps we could have a game some time," Eden put in, and Keira forced a smile.

"Perhaps," she said just as casually. Not likely, Mr Top Gun Cassidy, she declared under her breath, her eyes meeting his. And she suspected he knew exactly what she was thinking.

Eden glanced at his wristwatch, the flash of gold gleaming in the filtered sunlight, once again drawing Keira's attention to his strong, tanned hand. "Megan must have been held up. Daniel, could you go in and check with her? She may prefer Burton to take her something on a tray to have in the office."

Daniel frowned slightly and glanced quickly from Eden to Keira before he stood up and did as he had been bidden. For once Keira wished Daniel had defied his uncle because now she was left alone with Eden Cassidy. Again.

"Taking rather a chance, weren't you?" His deep voice made her start.

"A chance?" she repeated uncomprehendingly.

"Of wounding Daniel's fragile adolescent male ego by beating him on the court," he elaborated without intonation.

What a colossal chauvinist the man was. And how disparaging towards his nephew. Keira made herself take a mouthful of succulent ham before she replied with equal indifference.

"I think once again you've underestimated your nephew, Mr Cassidy. Surprisingly, Daniel doesn't have a problem with his self-image, which is quite amazing, considering..." Although Keira didn't complete the sentence the words hung as provocatively in the air as if she'd voiced them. Considering the fact he has a father-figure like you.

Eden set down his cutlery and sat back in his chair. "Considering?" he prompted through narrowed eyelids.

So he was calling her bluff.

Keira shrugged. "Considering the pressures put on young people today," she finished levelly, and had to suppress a surge of exhilarating excitement.

If she were honest she'd have to admit part of her was enjoying this verbal sparring.

One corner of his mouth twisted in a faint wry smile, his eyes acknowledging the point was hers. "Oh, yes. Peer pressure," he conceded.

"Peer pressure. Familial pressure. The pressure to succeed," Keira expanded. "It must be a great weight to bear sometimes."

"No doubt," he agreed. "But I think other generations have had just as much pressure. The pressures might have been slightly different but they were just as demanding. Didn't you suffer from as much social stress when you were Daniel's age?"

Keira glanced at him, trying to decide whether his reference to her age was a further slight on her relationship with his nephew. But she could glean nothing from his level expression.

"I guess I did. And I suppose the pressures were different," she confessed. "The desire to conform seems to be universal."

"I can't somehow see you as a conformist, Mrs Strong." He watched her like a jungle cat toying with his prey and Keira smiled wryly.

This prey would ensure she was more than a match for this particular predator. "You're mistaken again, Mr Cassidy. By no stretch of the imagination could I be called a rebel."

He raised one dark brow sceptically and Keira took a sip of cool water.

"I was boringly average and commonplace."

Eden also swallowed a mouthful of water and his lips quirked. "Every parent's dream child, hmm?"

She shrugged lightly. "I suppose so, depending on what you feel my parents would have expected of me."

"To find a young man, marry him and raise a family?" His gaze met hers in a silent challenge.

"Actually, they did," she said evenly, knowing it wasn't far from the truth. Her parents were in their early forties when she had surprised them by being born. They were both conservative in their outlook on the roles of men and women in society.

"And you went along with that?"

"In part." Keira dabbed her lips with her napkin. "I was married when I was twenty." And it was the biggest mistake of my life, she could have added. She had been so unworldly in some respects, torn between her yearning for a career and her parents' acceptance that she should marry Dennis. If she hadn't been so naïve—

"And talking again of marriage," Eden broke in on her tortured thoughts, "you still haven't filled me in on what the obviously trusting Mr Strong thinks about your weekend away with a male friend, a so much younger male friend?"

Keira blinked him back into focus. When Cassidy-Ford Publishing had bought out *Natural Life* magazine she had still been technically married to Dennis Strong. She'd seen no need to make any comments to anyone about their separation. Or Dennis's sudden death two years later.

"Dennis? He—" She stopped.

"Let me guess. He's a modern man. He understands," Eden Cassidy finished caustically for her, his lips twisting disparagingly. "Quite cosmopolitan and progressive. Or does he have his own distractions to keep him occupied?"

Their eyes met across the table and Keira held his gaze.

"My husband's dead, Mr Cassidy," she said evenly. "I've been a widow for three years. So," she continued when he made no immediate comment, "I suppose that makes my association with Daniel even more suspect. I mean, on past accusations I'd say you'd be the first to imply a frustrated widow on her own would have to be on the loose. Let's all lock up our sons.''

What he would have said in his defence, if he'd elected to defend himself, that was, Keira would never know for Daniel chose that moment to rejoin them.

''Burton's taken Megan a tray. She's waiting for a return call. Have you finished your lunch, Keira?'' he asked, and she nodded unsmilingly.

Daniel's gaze went from Keira to his uncle and back to Keira. He had to feel the tension that Keira knew arced between them, the incendiary vibrations that filled the air.

''OK. What say we walk off all this food?''

''Fine by me,'' Keira agreed. Anything to get away from Eden Cassidy.

''Great. Let me just make the rest of this into a sandwich and we can be off.''

''Mrs Strong may prefer to ride,'' his uncle suggested easily, and Daniel turned to Keira.

''Would you? I can have a couple of horses saddled in no time.''

''No, thanks, Daniel.'' Keira stood up. She hadn't been on a horse since she was a child and didn't fancy putting her rusty skills to the test today. She could just see herself falling off. With her luck it would probably be at Eden Cassidy's feet. ''I'd prefer a walk.''

''Fine. Let's go, then.'' Daniel took her arm and headed her down the steps past the glistening turquoise water of the swimming-pool.

And until they disappeared from sight she felt the piercing burn of Eden Cassidy's blue eyes running shivers down her spine.

Glancing ruefully at the deep marble spa bath and the vials of bath salts, Keira slipped out of her robe and under the shower. What she wouldn't give for a leisurely soak in the tub, but she knew she wouldn't have time for that luxury.

Letting the water play over her body, she wished this evening well and truly over. If she could only snap her fingers and find herself safely in her office immersed in her work on mid-Monday morning, with this deplorable situation behind her.

To think that Daniel's uncle could even imagine she could be involved with his nephew. It was ludicrous. But, she had to acknowledge, had she been the male and Daniel a young niece then the worst would have been conceded.

Sugar mummy? Keira bit off a giggle and then quickly sobered. The circumstances weren't funny at all. Now there was the party to get through, in the presence of the arrogant and insufferable Eden Cassidy.

During their long walk this afternoon Daniel had admitted his grandfather's party was going to be a rather large but very exclusive affair. Some four hundred guests were expected.

Keira stepped from the shower and wrapped the soft, warm bath-sheet around her. Well, in such a crowd, surely she could make herself invisible to Eden Cassidy. He'd be far too involved in circulating between his and Sir Samuel's family and friends to have time to seek her out to accuse her of further misdemeanours.

With some satisfaction she recalled the expression on his face when she'd informed him she was a widow. For one fleeting second she could have sworn he had been genuinely disconcerted. She arched her eyebrows at the mirror. Even if her statement had been only technically true.

She was a widow. But Dennis had been killed in a road accident just a week before their divorce became final.

Keira sighed and hung the bath-sheet on the heated gold towel rail. While she had the chance she should be enjoying such opulence where even the bath-towels made you feel pampered.

The carpet was soft beneath her feet as she walked through to the bedroom and slipped into her underwear. She glanced at the dress she'd chosen and grimaced slightly. Her one extravagance and it had stood her in good stead on the few occasions she'd had the opportunity to wear it.

The soft silky material slid over her shoulders and settled like a second skin. Keira nervously adjusted the bodice, checking the neckline. It was by no means plunging but it was lower than she usually wore, just hinting at the swell of firm, full breasts beneath.

She turned slightly to check the back of the dress that displayed even more smooth skin. There was no doubt that it suited her, she acknowledged. The steely grey colour lent her skin a creamy glow, accentuated the smoky grey of her eyes.

As usual she used little make-up, a touch of blue-grey eye-shadow, mascara on her lashes, lip gloss on her mouth. A fine gold locket which had belonged to her aunt clipped around her neck and nestled just above the beginning of the valley between her breasts. Then she brushed out her hair, tonight letting it fall to her shoulders in its natural waves instead of confining it in its usual chignon.

Slipping on her high-heeled shoes, she gave herself one final appraising look in the full-length mirror before telling herself she was as ready as she would ever be. And pray that she could elude the accusing and suspicious Eden Cassidy.

The ballroom of the palatial Cassidy mansion easily accommodated the four hundred guests Daniel had told Keira would be here to celebrate Sir Samuel Ford's eightieth birthday.

The old man himself was holding court at the other end of the room when Keira entered the wide doorway on Daniel's arm. Interested eyes turned as they paused on the top of the short flight of stairs leading down into the magnificent ballroom.

And Keira could imagine just what they might be thinking. That she was romantically involved with Sir Samuel's grandson and heir. His uncle wouldn't be the only one harbouring misconceptions. Her face flushed and she lowered her eyes nervously. Damn Daniel for talking her into this.

When she looked up her eyes went of their own accord to meet the cold gaze of Daniel's uncle. And the rest of the gathered guests simply faded into the shadowy background. Something fluttered into life in the pit of her stomach and her knees went decidedly weak. She was suddenly hot, and when Daniel spoke beside her she found her spinning mind couldn't compute his words.

The message that came through loudly and clearly was all purely physical. And it involved only Eden Cassidy.

Oh, no! Keira bit back a moan. This was absurd. She couldn't be attracted to such a man.

"Keira!" Daniel squeezed her arm and she broke the hold those implacable eyes had on her and turned her unfocused gaze on the younger man. "Keira?" Daniel frowned slightly, leaning closer to her, seemingly oblivious of the speculative glances cast their way. "Are you all right?"

"I'm fine," Keira hastened to assure him as she put more space between them.

He gave her one questioning glance before repeating his words. "Come and I'll introduce you to Sam."

Meeting Daniel's grandfather would be bad enough, but out of the corner of her eye she saw that Eden Cassidy had moved to join Sir Samuel Ford. If she went with Daniel now there'd be no escaping him.

Why had she…? She straightened her backbone. She only had herself to blame for getting herself into this situation so she might as well make the most of it. And that included Eden Cassidy. Her nerve-endings began to beat a wild tattoo and with no little effort she pulled herself together.

"Ready?" Daniel queried.

"Why not?" she said softly, and something in her tone brought a smile to Daniel's face.

Then he was moving them purposefully through the crowd towards the guest of honour.

"You know, just at this moment I could almost wish I were ten years older," Daniel said out of the corner of his mouth as he noticed a contemporary of his grandfather's running his eyes over Keira as they passed.

"Cool it, Daniel. Otherwise I doubt you'll see twenty, much less twenty-nine," Keira retaliated with barely a movement of her lips, and Daniel's grin broadened.

"I kid you not, Keira. You're the only woman I've met who really is as fantastic as she looks."

"High praise, Mrs Strong?" A cool voice stopped Daniel and Keira in their tracks.

CHAPTER THREE

"I WAS just going to introduce Keira to Sam," Daniel said defensively, and his uncle motioned that they accompany him towards the co-founder of Cassidy-Ford.

"Daniel!" Sam Ford wrapped his arms around his grandson and clapped him on the back.

"Happy birthday, Sam," Daniel said sincerely. "This do is a little ostentatious, isn't it?"

"Not a bit of it. Quite fitting for someone who's eighty years young." His grandfather laughed, his shrewd eyes taking in Keira as she stood tensely beside Eden Cassidy.

Daniel turned, but before he could make the introductions his uncle spoke.

"Sam, meet Keira Strong, Daniel's boss at *Chloe* magazine."

Daniel's jaw tightened as his gaze warred with Eden's.

"Pleased to meet you, Miss Strong." Sam took Keira's hand. "You know my daughter launched that magazine just before Daniel was born? It was her brainchild, as a matter of fact. She put it on the publishing map so I suppose it's only fitting that Daniel learns his ABC down there. I hear *Chloe*'s still ahead of its competitors."

"Yes. We seem to be keeping our hold on the top rung." Keira's tongue felt thick in her mouth, every nerve-ending so very aware of Eden Cassidy's hard body so close beside her.

"And I know that takes plain old hard work," Sam continued, his eyes going perceptively from Eden to his grandson and then back to Keira. "How long have you been part of *Chloe*'s team?"

"About five years."

Eden Cassidy moved slightly and the material of his suit jacket brushed against Keira's bare skin, making the hair on her arms stand on end. A shiver scurried from that transitory point of contact to blossom in the pit of her stomach and she shifted to disguise her reflex movement.

"She's a genius." Daniel's enthusiastic voice brought her attention slowly back from its erotic spree. "Works like a slave and expects us general dogsbodies to do the same. I daren't look as if I'm not busy or she finds me half a dozen things to be done. Honest, Sam."

"Your worst enemy is over-acting, Daniel," Eden said drily, and Sam chuckled.

"Your uncle and I told you it wouldn't be a bed of roses out there in the real world, Daniel."

"Ah, but I'm getting to smell the flowers, Sam," Daniel said with a smile, and his grandfather roared with laughter.

"And I'm dead green with envy. Especially since I never had a boss with legs like that."

Keira felt three pairs of masculine eyes rove over her and she raised her chin truculently.

Daniel met her stormy gaze and grinned sheepishly. "Another sexist comment like that, Sam, and I won't have a boss either. I'll be out on my proverbial ear."

"I don't do the hiring and firing, Daniel," Keira heard herself say pompously, and cringed at her superciliousness. Where had her sense of humour gone?

"Isn't that Bob and Jean just arriving?" Eden put in easily. "They're your godparents and you haven't seen them in ages, Daniel, so why don't you go with Sam to welcome them while Mrs Strong and I test out the band." He turned to Keira and held out his hand. "May I have the pleasure of this dance, Mrs Strong?"

Before Keira could decline his invitation she was in his

arms and he was guiding her expertly through the throng of dancers.

"Is it too late to refuse?" she asked him caustically, and his mouth twitched in a fleeting smile.

"Would you have?" His blue eyes gazed down at her and Keira almost missed her step. Eden Cassidy, of course, took her falter in his stride.

"For the record, yes. I would."

"Then it's fortunate I didn't wait for your crushing rejection."

His arm around her waist moved her imperceptibly closer to him and his hand was now resting on her bare back, fingertips nestling in the indentation of her spine. Keira's senses focused on his touch, felt the warmth that flared into full-blown fire. Her whole body grew hot and she knew high colour flooded her face.

The band chose that moment to change tempo and lapsed into a bracket of popular romantic ballads. As the mellow notes flowed about them Keira's perfidious soul seemed to be as one with his, and suddenly the intimacy of it made her knees want to fold beneath her.

Her breasts tingled where they brushed rhythmically against his hard chest, her nipples straining against the thin material of her bodice, her stomach muscles contracting as his thighs touched hers.

Eden Cassidy was an expert dancer and Keira's feet followed his lead as though they had been dancing together for years. In a previous life perhaps they had, as some believed.

Her eyes settled on her hand resting on his broad suit-clad shoulder, her skin pale against the dark material, and she realised that should she move that hand mere millimetres she would feel the taut muscles in his neck, that she would be free to caress the strands of dark hair resting on his nape.

She tore her gaze away, concentrating feverishly on the

innocuous knot of his tie. But then her mind's eye conjured up the movement of his strong hands adroitly folding that so very masculine accessory and her breathing became even more ragged. And her recalcitrant senses careered way out of control.

Of their own volition her grey eyes rose to the jut of his firm chin, to settle on his mouth. His lips were thin, the controlled line suggesting he rarely laughed, and the faint shadowy hollows beneath his high cheekbones made Keira wonder if he might sometimes neglect his health in pursuit of his business commitments.

At that moment he sidestepped her to avoid another couple, the instinctive movement drawing her impossibly closer to him, and her blood seemed to bolt through her veins with runaway recklessness. Her complete nervous system went on imperilled alert. Keira knew she couldn't have been more aware of him had they been naked, and she went cold and then hot again within the space of a split-second.

"You know, I haven't danced in years." Eden Cassidy's prosaic words ricocheted into Keira's lascivious thoughts, scattering them abruptly, and her eyes rose instantaneously to meet his in surprise.

The corners of his mouth lifted in a genuine smile, creating still more havoc with Keira's quivering nervous system, and the deep resonant sound of his soft laugh played over her with a million tiny titillations of her nerve endings.

The resulting clefts that bracketed his mouth changed his harsh features dramatically, and as he lifted his head his blue eyes sparkled beneath the light of the chandelier, making him inconceivably more heart-stoppingly attractive.

"Does your sceptical look mean you don't believe me, Mrs Strong?" That devastating smile still played around his mouth. "On my honour, it's quite true. I never seem to find the time. Do you suppose Daniel's right in repeatedly insisting I'm too wedded to my work?"

"Only you can answer that," Keira replied as evenly as

she could with her heartbeats still bouncing erratically in her breast. "But I should imagine Cassidy-Ford Publishing is a full-time job."

"It is that. But I have very competent staff and I do delegate. As I'm sure you do, Mrs Strong."

Keira glanced at him from beneath her lashes. Could he be fishing for information about the running of the magazine? Was he aware that Dianna filled less than her position on *Chloe*? Well, he wouldn't hear it from her, Keira thought firmly.

"Yes, I do delegate, but, as the editor, Dianna handles most of the work assignments. We all work very well as a team," she finished weakly, part of her wishing her editor hadn't put her in such a position.

"So where do you see *Chloe* going in the next year or so?"

"Going?" she repeated in surprise. "In exactly the direction it has been, I would have thought. And I don't mean standing still. The magazine constantly flexes with the needs of its readers. While it's so successful, why alter the format—or the staff?" she added quickly, recalling the supposition caused by the appearance of the time-and-motion study man Daniel had reminded her about.

Eden's eyes had narrowed on her. "You think that's what I plan on doing?"

Keira shrugged. "I have no idea, although there have been a few rumours," she said carefully. "But I feel I should repeat what I said. Why interfere with a successful enterprise? Our staff work well together and I wouldn't want to see that changed in any way."

"Loyal, too," he said quietly and grimaced. "Is there no end to your virtues, Mrs Strong?"

"What...what do you mean?" Keira swallowed nervously, feeling the timbre of the conversation shift just fractionally, giving it that heady sense of danger once again.

"Obviously competent at her job. Loyal to her staff. As

well as being—how did Daniel describe you?—a woman who's as fantastic as she looks.''

Keira flushed. ''I take pride in doing my job well,'' she began haughtily, highly embarrassed by the turn of the dialogue.

''Oh, I know you do, Mrs Strong. My—'' he paused and raised one dark brow ''—snoops weren't wrong about that.''

Their eyes met, held. Cool steel-blue and steady smoky grey. Keira's were the first to fall.

''I guess I should apologise for that.'' She fought to keep her voice dispassionately normal. ''But I was provoked, wouldn't you say?''

''What happened to your husband?'' he asked quietly, and his change of subject and the concern in his tone tore down Keira's defences.

''He was killed in a car accident,'' she replied flatly.

''It must have been difficult for you.''

''Yes. I...'' Keira sighed. ''Dennis and I were separated at the time. We had been for a couple of years. But it was still a terrible shock.''

They danced in silence for a moment, each lost in their own thoughts. Keira tried to bring Dennis's face into focus but his boyish features blurred in the process. Dennis had been handsome, but weak. So totally different from the man whose strong arms held her in his grasp. With flawless timing Keira's body reminded her of the rock-hard wall of Eden's chest, his long legs, and... There was, she admitted resignedly, no contest.

But what was she doing making a comparison anyway? she asked herself angrily. It wasn't as though she had ever been interested in replacing Dennis. And if she had been, there was no way she would consider a man as high-powered, as prominently profiled as Eden Cassidy. She'd have to be insane. Wouldn't she?

Keira pulled her wayward thoughts to a jarring halt. A

man like Eden Cassidy would have no interest in an average-looking nobody like her.

She glanced up at him again and the look in his blue eyes that split-second before he masked his thoughts belied her speculation. She knew in that revealing moment that she did hold some interest for him.

Keira swallowed quickly, her mind trying to rein in her galloping senses. Interested he may be but she'd lay bets his concern wasn't altruistic, but brutally obvious.

Eden Cassidy, head of the prestigious and prosperous Cassidy-Ford Publishing and Keira Strong, assistant editor and virtual employee. One of thousands. Keira could almost laugh. It sounded like a fairy-tale. And she'd given up believing in them a long time ago. Nor was she even vaguely interested in indulging in a sordid affair with a wealthy libertine.

She had to get away from him. Where was Daniel? Her eyes ran over the crowd around them and only then did she notice even more speculative looks slid furtively their way. And she could imagine just what they were all thinking of her now. First the nephew, now the uncle. She must be providing a banquet of food for gossipy thoughts. She'd have to excuse herself.

At that moment she spotted Daniel through a break in the crowd. He was craning his neck above the dancers and, catching sight of Keira and his uncle, he began to make his way towards them.

A slight frown furrowed his brow when he reached them and he looked quickly from one to the other.

"Megan's looking for you," he told his uncle without preamble. "Something about a fax from New York or something. It sounded important," he added quickly, for good measure.

Eden grimaced and slowly, far too slowly as far as Keira was concerned, he relinquished his hold on her and gave her a slight bow. "Duty calls," he said derisively. "I'll leave you in Daniel's capable hands. For now,'' he added softly, for Keira's ears only, as he turned and left them.

Keira danced with Daniel, who seemed just a little less exuberant, a trifle more subdued. Or so it appeared to Keira, who had to acknowledge she now felt much the same. However, during the course of the evening he politely introduced her to his family and some of his uncle's and grandfather's friends.

At supper, as lavish an affair as the rest of the celebration had been, Daniel attentively plied her with delicious food and the one glass of the very best champagne she allowed herself.

Eden Cassidy circulated conscientiously, Keira knew, for her body seemed automatically tuned to his movements about the large ballroom. Throughout the evening she would find herself beginning to relax and then he would cross her line of vision, or their eyes would meet through a break in the crowd, and her muscles would tense involuntarily. And not for the first time she fervently wished the evening well and truly over.

The only time Eden had taken to the dance-floor had been with Keira, and just when she was convinced she was to have the dubious honour of being his only dancing partner she saw him guiding the tall and impeccably gowned Megan Donnelly on to the floor.

They made a striking couple. In her high heels, with her hair piled on top of her head in a smooth chignon, Megan was almost as tall as Eden, and as Keira watched, unable to draw her gaze away, they spoke softly and easily to each other as they danced.

Yet they didn't look as though they fitted together. Somehow the picture wouldn't jell. Not those cold blue eyes paired with that controlled, willow-slim body. Keira found herself trying to imagine Eden and Megan in a passionate embrace and the picture that was conjured up did nothing to waylay the icy little knot in her stomach as it grew tentacles that reached up to squeeze her heart.

No! Keira remonstrated with herself again. She couldn't be so foolish. And she couldn't allow this nonsensical fantasy to develop any further. Eden Cassidy was way out of her league and she didn't want or need the resulting turmoil such ridiculousness would definitely engender.

"Hey, Dan! Cat! How's it doing?" A young voice broke in on Keira and Daniel as they stood talking, having decided to take a break from the dancing for a while.

They both turned as the young man, obviously a contemporary of Daniel's, joined them. His jaw dropped comically as Keira faced him and he realised his mistake.

"Oh, sorry. You look just like... Um, I thought you were someone else," he mumbled. "Thought it was funny Cat was here. Oh." He stopped talking, his expression registering what had apparently been a warning look from Daniel.

Keira bit back a smile as Daniel heartily made the introductions.

"Keira, this is Rick Jansen, a friend of mine. Rick, meet my boss, Keira Strong."

"Your boss. Wow! Um, pleased to meet you." Rick shook hands with Keira, his admiring eyes moving surreptitiously over her. "So old Dan really does have a job?"

"Yes, I'm afraid he does. At the moment," she added teasingly for Daniel's benefit.

"I'll need to see it to believe it," Rick continued. "And you're his boss? Um, any vacant positions going?"

"None you could handle," Daniel gibed back. "Ignore him, Keira. No class." He glanced at his wristwatch. "And only four or five hours late. That should tell us something."

"Car trouble." Rick shrugged. "Still, we thought we'd at least wish Sam all the best before we headed back to the city. And apart from that, I'm starving. Gina—my girl-friend," he added for Keira's information, "is scrounging us some leftovers so I'd better go find her. Catch you later, Dan. OK?''

He disappeared as suddenly as he had appeared and Keira turned back to an obviously disconcerted Daniel.

"Gee, is it hot in here? Or is it just me?" He loosened his tie. "What say we get some air?"

"I'm fine, Daniel," Keira began and he looked at her imploringly.

"Ten minutes, Keira. And I need some company." He took her arm and led her through the open double doors out on to the wide, brightly lit patio.

They strolled over to the cement parapet and leant against the still-warm balustrade. Two large potted umbrella trees threw shadow about them, partially obscuring them from the doorway.

"Nice and cool out here, isn't it?" Daniel said, his voice a little uneasy, and Keira sighed.

"Lovely," she said pointedly.

"I'd give anything to get out of this monkey suit," Daniel hurried on, undoing the button at his collar. "Give me casual dress any day. Or night."

"But not at your grandfather's celebration, which," Keira added, "he seems to be enjoying immensely."

Daniel relaxed a little and laughed. "Sam always does. And how about you, Keira? It hasn't been as bad as you thought it would be, has it?"

"No. I suppose not," Keira replied carefully. Apart from those earth-shattering moments in Eden Cassidy's arms. And the continuing earth-shattering moments that followed at regular intervals.

"Aren't you glad I asked you? Or is that going a bit far?"

Keira laughed softly. "Perhaps. But I'm still hazy about *why* you asked me. And it wasn't because you could talk to me like a sister, was it? Or to pique your uncle, I hope."

"No. Not that. Well, not exactly. I did ask you because I felt we get on pretty well and..." Daniel stopped and sighed. "I suppose I do owe you an explanation. I'm just not sure where to start. It's sort of complicated, you see."

"Would it help if I asked the sixty-four-thousand-dollar question?" Keira said perceptively. "So who's Cat?"

"Just a friend." Daniel shrugged and Keira sensed in the semi-darkness that he was going pink about the ears. When Keira made no comment he shot a sideways glance at her and she shook her head.

"Something tells me she's much more than that, but far be it from me to invade your privacy."

"It's not that, Keira. It's just..." Daniel stopped again and sighed loudly. "I met Cat at an inter-school debating contest when we were sixteen. Actually, she's a month older than me. I told you I prefer older women! And she does look a lot like you, which is how Rick came to put his foot in his mouth in there. Cat has fair hair, same length as yours, but her eyes are sort of hazel."

"And she wouldn't come tonight so you chose me as the look-alike substitute?" Keira shook her head. "I'm not sure I like that, Daniel. And you're taking quite a chance, aren't you? What if the elusive Cat finds out?"

"You weren't a substitute, Keira. Not the way you mean." Daniel defended himself. "And Cat knows about you."

"I see. So this is a modern romance?" she teased, and when Daniel would have protested she held up her hand. "I'm sorry, Daniel. That was a low blow. Perhaps you'd best finish your tale of woe."

"This is serious, Keira." Daniel assured her. "And you really are like her. Not just in looks. She's intelligent, funny, straightforward. She doesn't play games. Cat's always Cat. We've been going out together on and off for about two years."

"Then why didn't you bring her to the party tonight?"

"You answered that before. She didn't want to come."

Keira raised her eyebrows.

"We—that is, you see, she isn't keen on meeting my uncle."

"No?" Keira could sympathise with the girl. Or so she told herself.

"No. And Eden wouldn't be overjoyed at meeting her," Daniel added despondently.

"Why not? I'm sure you're underestimating your uncle," Keira heard herself add, and began to feel just a little hypocritical. Not hours ago she'd been convinced she'd believe anything about the arrogant Eden Cassidy. She was changing sides in the middle of the round. Except it wasn't a game. "Unless Cat's one of the giggling air-head brigade."

"Give it a rest, Keira." Daniel pulled a face. "And trust me on this. Eden would blow a fuse. Remember that strike on the *Daily Post* six months ago when the delivery guys went out?"

"What could that possibly have to do with you and Cat?" Keira asked, perplexed. "Unless she delivers your uncle's newspapers," she couldn't help adding lightly.

"Of course she doesn't," Daniel said testily. "She's at uni. But who did all the negotiating?"

She frowned. "Doug Craigie, wasn't it?"

"The same. And the dispute before that? Doug Craigie. My uncle's arch-enemy." Daniel paused melodramatically. "And Cat's father."

Keira straightened. "I see. And you've kept your relationship with Cat Craigie from your uncle and, I take it, her father, for three years?"

Daniel nodded. "It hasn't been easy." He hoisted himself on to the balustrade, letting his hands dangle dejectedly between his knees. "Not that Cat's afraid of meeting Eden. Hell, she's the most courageous, most honourable person I know, apart from you, Keira. But she doesn't want to start anything. I mean, Eden and Doug Craigie were at each other's throats for days the last time."

"But they sorted it out in the end, quite amicably," Keira reminded him.

"Yes, well, Cat and I would rather keep ourselves out of it."

"If you care about this girl, Daniel, then your uncle's going to have to know eventually. You must see that."

"I know, Keira. And I am serious about Cat, you can believe that. She's the only girl I've ever been really interested in and I see myself with her for the rest of our lives. But she's just so damn stubborn about this." Daniel shook his head despondently and Keira reached out and patted his shoulder.

"Although I don't particularly care to be used as a smokescreen I think I understand, Daniel, and I'm sorry. Perhaps you should just leave it for now. I'm sure you'll know when the time's right to explain it to your family."

Daniel nodded and pushed himself into a standing position, turning to Keira with a crooked smile. "I feel a lot better talking about it. Thanks." He took Keira's hand in his. "You know, another time, another place, you and I..." He stopped and Keira smiled.

"I understand, Daniel. And I admire you for recognising the difference," she said softly. "You're an exceptional young man."

Daniel raised her hand to his lips.

At the sound of measured footsteps on the tiled patio Daniel dropped Keira's hand and they both swung around as Eden Cassidy approached them. The harsh outdoor light was behind him, throwing his features into shadow, making his expression unreadable.

Keira stiffened and for short seconds that seemed like long minutes no one spoke. Then Daniel moved beside Keira and broke into hurried speech.

"We were hot. From dancing. We came out for some air."

Sympathising with Daniel's awkwardness, Keira shifted

her weight from one foot to the other, bringing her closer to the younger man, and she put her hand compassionately on his back. And she sensed Eden Cassidy was completely aware of her movement.

"It is quite warm, isn't it?" Eden said easily. "It's surprising you've got the patio all to yourselves."

"We were about to go back inside—" Daniel had recovered his composure "—if you're ready, Keira?"

"Sure." Keira would have moved forward but Eden Cassidy stood his ground, directly in front of her, effectively cornering her between Daniel and the potted umbrella trees. She'd have to brush past him or make a show of stepping carefully around him.

"The party's going well," Daniel remarked, a little more at ease now that his uncle seemed to be no threat to him, and Keira had to repress the urge to push Daniel towards the doorway so that she could escape the unsettling presence of the tall man standing intimidatingly in front of her.

"Yes," Eden replied perfunctorily as Daniel began to walk across the patio, with Keira right behind him.

"Oh, Mrs Strong." Eden's words stopped them both. "I'd like a few words with you. If you'll excuse us, Daniel." He dismissed his nephew.

Daniel's chin rose. "I'll wait."

"I want to discuss business with your boss," Eden said unperturbed. "Privately."

"Look, Eden." Daniel faced him. "If you're going to talk to Keira about me then I'm going to stay."

"There you are, Dan," Rick Jansen called from the doorway. "Gina and I are heading off. Think you could come and help me start my car? Battery's a bit iffy so I'll probably need a push to get it going."

"Go on, Daniel," his uncle said firmly. "We'll see you inside."

With a muttered exclamation Keira couldn't catch, and

was relieved she didn't, Daniel ungraciously joined his friend.

"A rather propitious interruption," Eden Cassidy remarked, and moved to lean his hip against the balustrade where his nephew had been sitting.

"How could you do that to Daniel?" Keira asked him before she could stop herself.

"Do what?" he countered easily.

"Embarrass him. Come out here to check up on him. Spy," she finished harshly, and he raised one arrogant dark brow. "But on past experience I don't know why I'm surprised."

"You don't? Why so, Mrs Strong?"

"Your bogus time-and-motion study henchman at the magazine last week for one."

"You're misconstruing, Mrs Strong. Jonesy—" he pulled a wry face "—Ken Jones, who's worked for me for more years than I care to recall, was exactly what he said he was and his appearance had nothing to do with Daniel."

Keira watched him, her brain turning over the implications of his words. Was Eden Cassidy planning on firing some of the staff at *Chloe*? she wondered again. And if so, who? She bit her lip. The magazine was running smoothly and efficiently as it was.

"But I didn't come out here to discuss the magazine or to keep what you've assured me are unnecessary tabs on my nephew," he continued. "I wanted to talk to you about a different matter, associated, but detached."

Keira stood silently, her intuition suddenly setting warning ringing, some sixth sense telling her she wasn't going to find anything to like in this different matter, associated or detached.

"It does concern Daniel and I want to restate my caution about your association with my nephew."

"Mr Cassidy," Keira began, wanting to end the conversation before it got any worse. And she had an awful premonition it was about to do just that.

"As you know," he continued as though she hadn't spoken, "I'm strongly against my nephew's involvement in a heavy affair at this stage. Not that there isn't something to be said in favour of a young man sowing his wild oats with an experienced older woman.

"However, Daniel doesn't need complications of that kind distracting him when he should be concentrating on preparing for his university studies. So I want to suggest a solution."

Was he going to offer her money? Keira wondered, as an ominous dread took hold of her.

"You are an experienced woman, Mrs Strong, wouldn't you say?"

Keira felt a flood of red course from her throat to her cheeks. Surely he...?

Deliberately he pushed himself upright, away from the balustrade, standing to face her, far, far too close to her. "You could use your—" he paused slightly "—time to better advantage. I assure you, I'd see you wouldn't regret it. I'm an experienced man. Why waste your time with a boy?"

CHAPTER FOUR

STRANGELY, some small part of Keira stood off from her, curiously unruffled, watching this unbelievable dialogue. That same part was aware of nearby music from the ballroom mingling with the hum of conversations, heard the leaves of the potted umbrella trees rustling in the gentle breeze, registered that they were casting shifting shadows over the scene she knew would be burned into her memory.

She couldn't believe he'd said what he had and her jaw slackened in dismay. Had her ears deceived her? Was Eden Cassidy blatantly propositioning her? No, surely not. A man in his position wouldn't presume to, would he?

"I...I beg your pardon?" she got out at last as he continued to gaze down at her, his expression inscrutable in the shadows effected by the light behind his broad-shouldered body.

"You seem to have some trouble understanding me, Mrs Strong. I thought I enunciated quite clearly, so what's the problem?" He made a slight, irritated movement of his hand and Keira pulled herself into some semblance of self-control.

"Oh, I heard what you said, Mr Cassidy, and please don't bother repeating it," she added quickly. "I was merely giving you the chance to apologise for your offensive offer, which I'm sure you don't expect me to take seriously."

"On the contrary, Mrs Strong. I've never been more serious in my life."

The cool of the night breeze touched Keira's skin and she

shivered slightly. "And I don't believe you, Mr Cassidy. If this is some kind of sick joke then it doesn't flatter you in the least. How can you make such a blatantly unconscionable proposition to someone you've known for less than twenty-four hours? It's...it's obscene."

"Come now, Mrs Strong. You're an extremely attractive woman. You don't need me to tell you that. So why underestimate the power of those very obvious attractions?" he inquired indolently.

"Obvious..." Keira's teeth closed on the word and lips twisted in disgust. "I assure you I'm well aware of my attractions, Mr Cassidy, and I also have no illusions regarding their limitations, so I feel I should warn you that any patronisation in that direction is going to be pointless. Only a fool wouldn't see that this all comes back to Daniel's and my phantom relationship."

"And you're not a fool, Mrs Strong," he put in levelly as Keira's anger churned inside her.

"I've already informed you in no uncertain terms that there is no relationship between Daniel and myself. I can't be any clearer than that," she continued directly. "So there's absolutely no necessity to extend yourself to such extravagant lengths to warn me off."

"I'd be lying if I didn't admit that I find the thought of such a relationship between you and my nephew abhorrent, but I assure you I'm not in the habit of offering myself up as a sacrifice every time Daniel decides to date. I'm not into masochism. Which leaves us one other intriguing possibility. Have you considered my intentions might not be as selfless as you appear to think they are?" He paused. "Perhaps I'm interested."

Keira's muscles tensed until she feared they'd snap under the strain. "Interested?" she repeated a little breathily.

He inclined his dark head slightly and the light momentarily reflected the bright sparkle of his eyes.

Keira reined in her fervent imagination as it threatened to

take the heady thought and make a wild, impassioned dash with it. Interested in her? No! She couldn't allow it.

"Well, Mr Cassidy, I'm not," she stated firmly, surprising herself with her resolve.

"No?" As he lifted his dark head the artificial illumination now caught one side of his face, the sweep of his hard jawline, played over the hollow beneath his cheekbone. "Are you sure of that, Mrs Strong?"

"Sure?" she echoed with considerably less conviction, and when she heard her uncertainty she raised her chin determinedly. "Of course I'm sure. I barely know you, for heaven's sake."

"An obstacle that could be quickly, easily and enjoyably overcome," he stated matter-of-factly.

Keira felt the flutter of her pulse in her throat and turned slightly away from him, folding her arms protectively about herself. "Not from where I stand," she replied sarcastically.

"Then perhaps you aren't standing in the right place. It would be a simple matter of taking one step in this direction."

Keira swung back to face him, disproportionately piqued by his levity. Had he moved closer to her? She was sure he had. An electrifying fear clutched at her and she took a quick steadying breath. "Look, Mr Cassidy, I'm afraid I don't find getting to know a stranger, in the sense you mean, something that can be achieved quickly or easily. And as to the enjoyable—well, that remains to be seen," she finished lamely.

"But you've already seen it," he said quietly, his low voice playing over her susceptible senses before she had time to build a defence against his evocatively erotic tone.

"I—" Keira swallowed "—I don't know what you mean."

"When we were dancing. The sparks were there. You were as aware of them as I was. Weren't you, Keira?"

His husky voice saying her Christian name so intimately

was almost her undoing. Keira. No one had said it quite like
that before. It flowed over her tingling skin like smooth silk,
teasing each nerve ending into instantaneous arousal.

With an exhilarating sense of vertigo she felt her body
begin to capitulate, to incline towards his. He was the hunter
and she his quarry. He was the burning light and she the
moth. And her mind screamed out her danger, warned of
the destructive singe of wings that might very well result
from venturing too close to his fateful flame.

"You're mistaken, Mr Cassidy," she assured him icily
with what little composure remained unmoved by his tantalising magnetism. "And I'm surprised that you could be
so fanciful."

He laughed softly and Keira's knees went weak.

"So. You think I have a vivid imagination?" he said
wryly. "And perhaps I do, in certain—" he paused explic-
itly "—intimate situations. But I don't think I was—am—
misconstruing the attraction that exists between us."

With an exclamation of disgust Keira turned her back on
him again. "I think this ridiculous conversation has gone
far enough. I repeat, Mr Cassidy, I am not interested."

"And I, Mrs Strong, am definitely," he said with low
conviction, "interested."

"Why me?" Keira asked at last into the heavy silence
that stretched between them, gathering its own volatile mo-
mentum.

"Why not? I meant it when I said I find you a very
attractive woman."

Keira fancied she felt the brush of his breath on the back
of her neck and she wanted to run for her life. But her
uncooperative legs refused to carry her away to safety. "Oh,
curse my fatal charm," she got out bitingly, and he made
no immediate comment.

And the silence stretched between them until Keira had
to break its potent hold. "Attractive women in your circles

are a dime a dozen,'' she threw at him, like a drowning person clutching at a proffered lifesaver.

"You're intelligent—''

Keira sighed loudly. "Intelligent? If I had any sense at all I'd be slapping your face and leaving you to try out your distasteful line on someone else.'' She moved agitatedly back to face him. "And slapping your face, incidentally, is growing far more appealing to me by the minute.''

"Then I suggest you reconsider. I'm a stickler for the equality of the sexes. I'd slap you back.''

Keira felt his eyes lock steadily with her own, felt their strength of purpose in spite of the shadowy light. She suspected he'd carry out his intentions, too.

Eden Cassidy represented all that was mysteriously forbidden, a walk over uncertain ground, an untravelled path that held a tempting unknown. But it all led to a world she'd visited before and her experience had not been a happy one. She had no desire to go through the pain again, she reminded herself.

Yet the temptation was there, glowing like a welcoming beacon in the dark. It would only take one step. But Keira knew she couldn't take it. Not on the terms he was offering.

"Equality of the sexes.'' It was Keira's turn to laugh. "Next thing you'll be telling me you're sensitive, caring and vulnerable. Now, why can't I picture you in that role? Maybe because you like playing to the gallery too much.''

"You think I'm theatrical?'' He raised dark brows and Keira shrugged.

"I think you also enjoy playing the field.''

He gave a soft, nerve-honing laugh. "So I flit from flower to flower?''

"Precisely,'' Keira said sarcastically.

"You should know not to believe everything you read in the glossies,'' he countered, moving imperceptibly, yet enough for Keira's acutely vigilant senses to react, tensing her muscles in reflex defence. "I'm a one-woman-at-a-time man. Always have been. A woman always knows she has my complete and undivided attention.''

''Nice sentiments. But only for as long as it lasts, I'd say. Well, I just don't intend to be the latest blossom for you to add to your bunch. Now, I've really had enough of this conversation. I'm a little tired and I'm going inside.''

''Running away, Keira?'' His words stopped her immediately. ''I thought you'd enjoy a challenge.'' His fingers settled on her shoulder, searing her through the fabric of her dress, and she jumped like a startled colt.

''I'm not playing power games, Mr Cassidy. And no means no in my language,'' she made herself add bitingly, looking meaningfully down at his hand on her upper arm.

'''No' is not what your body language is saying to me,'' he said softly, his fingers sliding down her arm, his thumb gently teasing the soft inner skin of her elbow.

Keira's physical response to his touch rose almost to choke her and she was just as suddenly terribly afraid of the strength of her reaction, of the knowledge that she didn't want to reject him.

''I can't believe this.'' She made herself snatch her arm from his hold. ''Only hours ago I wasn't good enough for your precious nephew and now you're lowering yourself and your lofty standards to take me on yourself. You're either selling yourself cheaply or you're desperate. Neither of which I am, fortunately. I told you before I don't sleep around. I never have—''

''I don't recall implying you did,'' he cut in concisely.

''And I don't intend to start now with you,'' Keira continued, the bit well and truly between her teeth. ''No matter how—'' she paused, regarding him scathingly from head to toe ''—impressive your credentials are. So, to correct any misapprehension you may be under, let's use some old but straightforward clichés. Don't call me, I'll call you. Goodnight, Mr Cassidy. Oh, and I wouldn't hold my breath waiting for the phone to ring if I were you.''

With that Keira marched back into the ballroom, not looking back to see if he was following her. Once back inside she went in search of Daniel and pleaded tiredness, retiring to spend a sleepless night in the opulent bedroom. And when Daniel and Keira appeared for a late brunch the next morning Burton informed them that Eden and Megan had already left to return to the city.

After a perfunctory knock on the office door Keira's assistant walked in waving a newspaper around in front of her, and Keira sighed resignedly. At this rate she'd never get any work done.

Daniel had already interrupted her unnecessarily and it was hard enough keeping her errant thoughts from drifting to other, more regrettably disturbing incidents, without these intermittent intrusions.

"How long have we known each other, Keira?" Roxie Denahey demanded without the usual preliminaries as she tossed her well-proportioned frame into the chair in front of Keira's desk. The chair creaked in protest.

"Do you really want me to admit out loud that it's been over twenty years?" Keira asked with a faint smile. She and Roxie had attended primary school together.

"Twenty years, Keira Strong. And you can't even tell me, can't even breathe so much as a whisper, when something momentous happens in your life." Roxie frowned disgruntledly.

"This is a particularly momentous something, I take it?" Keira raised her eyebrows. "You know what an exciting life I lead, Roxie, so would you care to give me a hint about which significant event I've failed to give you details of, thus maliciously ruffling your sensitive feathers?"

"Which significant event?" Roxie scowled. "This one." She fluttered the newspaper. "Featured all over the social pages of the Sunday paper."

Keira's heart sank. It had to be Sir Samuel's party. She

hadn't given a thought to the public interest such a distinguished occasion would generate. Or, until this moment, recalled the camera flashes. But in her defence, she had had other things on her mind. Like Eden Cassidy. And his outrageous proposition. Keira almost groaned.

"Don't tell me you haven't seen it?" Roxie's voice rose in disbelief. "Good grief! You haven't!" she exclaimed at Keira's expression. "Well, let me be the first to flash it by you."

Reluctantly Keira took the newspaper from the other girl and glanced down at the grainy photographs. Then she did groan out loud.

One photograph was larger than the six or seven others. And it immediately drew attention. Any photograph of Eden Cassidy's incredibly rugged good looks would, Keira acknowledged.

However, it wasn't simply a shot of Eden Cassidy. He was in the photograph, looking as attractive as he always did. And so was Sir Samuel Ford, smiling broadly at the camera, his arm around his only grandson.

But on his right stood a reasonably tall woman with shoulder-length fair hair, a heart-shaped face and a firm chin. The photographer had caught that chin as its owner lifted it with a hint of tenacity as she gazed levelly into the lens.

"Newsy little caption under the photo, too," Roxie remarked and recited it off pat. "Helping to celebrate Sir Samuel Ford's eightieth birthday were his grandson, Daniel Ford Cassidy (right), Eden Cassidy (left) and Keira Strong. Eden Cassidy is the younger son of William Cassidy, Sir Samuel's late partner and co-founder of the Cassidy-Ford media conglomerate. Keira Strong is the assistant editor of the family company's highly successful *Chloe* magazine."

Keira's eyes were drawn from her own features to those of the man standing so close beside her, so close that their shoulders appeared to be pressing together. Keira moved in her chair to disguise the sudden quiver that began in the pit of her stomach and rose to set her skin tingling. Almost as if Eden Cassidy were touching her again.

"I didn't even know we'd been photographed," she said a little breathily.

"Shucks! And *I* didn't even know you'd been invited to the social bash of the year," Roxie stated mockingly.

"You were away last week and Daniel didn't ask me to go with him until Thursday," Keira began to explain.

"Daniel?" Roxie's mouth fell open in amazement. "Daniel Cassidy? Are you putting me on?"

"Of course not. Would I dare?" Keira threw back quickly.

"Our young, our very young Daniel Cassidy?" Roxie continued as though Keira hadn't spoken.

"Daniel asked me to go with him as a favour."

"You had a date with—"

"Roxie, please," Keira appealed. "It wasn't a date. He needed someone to go with him to his grandfather's party and I, well, I agreed. End of story." *End of story*? A mocking voice inside her laughed at her blatant distortion of the truth.

"Daniel!" Roxie repeated. "And here I was fantasising that while my back was turned you'd been whisked off by Eden Cassidy, the heart-throb of the social set."

"Are you kidding, Roxie?" Keira's heartbeats performed their recklessly uninhibited dance yet again, as if their cue was simply the mention of Eden Cassidy's name. What would her friend think if she told her about that very same Eden Cassidy's preposterous proposition?

"If I'd known you were interested in younger men—" Roxie began, but Keira quelled her friend with a constraining look.

Briefly subdued, Roxie gazed at Keira for long moments and then she sighed. "How long have I been working with you, Keira?"

"More twenty questions?" Keira asked quizzically and shook her head in capitulation, knowing Roxie wouldn't let it rest until she'd had her say. "About ten years, including the last five years on *Chloe*."

"OK. I do know you pretty well, don't I? I've been with you through thick and thin, marriage and divorce. So tell me, in the three years since Dennis died how many dates have you had?"

"Quite a few," Keira began defensively and Roxie pulled a face.

"A few is right. I'd say you've been lucky to average two a year." She held up her plump hand and ticked off on her fingers. "There was that cowboy. That fizzled out, thank heavens."

"I didn't want to move to the country and he didn't want to settle in the city. It was a mutual decision to part," Keira told her.

"Then there was the lawyer with no sense of humour," Roxie continued. "And the computer guy who was only interested in your chips rather than your whole circuit."

Keira laughed. "There's no need for the roll-call, Roxie. I haven't lost any sleep over any of them."

"That's precisely your problem. Honestly, Keira, don't you sometimes yearn to go to bed for something other than sleep?" Roxie sat back in the chair and grinned at Keira's embarrassed discomposure.

"Is this any way to talk to your boss?" Keira asked with mock seriousness and Roxie rolled her eyes.

"I'm not wearing my assistant-to-the-assistant-editor's cap at the moment. Right now I've got on my friend-of-long-standing hat. And I won't be sidetracked. You can blush all you want, but haven't I gone right to the seat of your problem?"

Keira grimaced. "I see no problem. Shall we just say I've deprogrammed that part of my life? And are you speaking from experience, Roxie?" Keira tried once again to deflect the course of the conversation knowing she had next to no chance of success.

"Now, don't try to distract me. This is a 'do as I say, not as I do' lecture. So can I make one tiny suggestion for you to consider?"

"Would it make any difference if I said no?" Keira quickly held up her hand. "And don't even think of taking that the wrong way."

"Would I do that?" Roxie widened her eyes innocently. "Look, just give a bit of thought to getting your unused programme into running order. Just in case."

"I know I'll regret this, but in case of what?"

"In case Eden Cassidy offers you some wonderfully forbidden fruit."

"You sound like a pop song." Keira tried to laugh lightly. "And I'm not into forbidden fruit."

"If Eden Cassidy—no, I'll rephrase that," Roxie continued. "When Eden Cassidy, and I say when because the man *is* interested—"

"Roxie, you're being absurd," Keira cut in, swallowing the rush of excited anticipation she was too slow to quell. Her friend was inadvertently skating far too close to the truth.

"Rubbish! Take a look at that photograph. You mark my words, Keira. That man is interested."

Keira shifted uneasily. If Roxie only knew...

"And when he holds out the shiny red apple," her friend was continuing, "I don't want to hear you've refused to take a bite."

"Not the best of analogies," Keira remarked wryly and Roxie leant across and picked up the newspaper again.

"Oh, I don't know, Keira. I'd say it was spot on. I mean, the man's poetry, pure poetry." She shook her head. "All I can say is, his mother must have known something when she named him Eden because he's the closest thing to paradise I've ever seen."

Keira didn't know whether to laugh or be angry with Roxie, but she was saved from having to make a decision when her office door opened again.

"Can you believe it's Monday already?" Dianna Forester, the editor of *Chloe*, strode into the room. "I spent the weekend on Tommy's yacht and I'm totally exhausted."

"And a good time was had by all, by the look of you," Roxie remarked ironically. "With you two and your adventures I feel as though my weekend of gardening and household chores absolutely pales into insignificance."

Dianna's eyes turned sharply to Keira. "Well, I know I've been partying, but what have you been up to, Keira?"

"What indeed?" Roxie held out the newspaper and Dianna took it from her, her eyes narrowing as she glanced at the photograph Roxie pointed out to her.

"You went to Sir Samuel's party? I didn't know you were on such close terms with the family," she said carefully and Keira shrugged.

"I'm not. I went with Daniel, as a favour."

"Would that I were asked such a favour," Roxie put in expressively.

"It was a last-minute thing," Keira began, wondering gloomily how long she was going to have to suffer the fallout from allowing Daniel to talk her into going to that wretched party.

"And what with one thing and another—" Roxie shifted in her chair to look back at Keira "—I forgot to ask you if you heard anything over the weekend to substantiate the epidemic of rumours about staff shuffling here on the magazine. Did Eden Cassidy drop any hints to you?"

Keira shook her head and Dianna pursed her lips thoughtfully.

"I suppose you could scarcely raise the subject over dinner," she said, giving Keira another piercing look. "No doubt we'll hear all soon enough. Well, I've got stacks to do myself so I'll get to it.'' Dianna replaced the newspaper on Keira's desk and left.

"That will be a first,'' Roxie muttered caustically.

"I should finish this, too,'' Keira said quickly, before Roxie could continue. "Put it around that I don't want any more interruptions, until lunchtime at least.''

Roxie stood up. "Methinks that includes me. No trouble. I'll see you later, now that you've shamed me into putting my nose to the grindstone. And, Keira, do me a favour and at least consider my advice.''

After Roxie left Keira tried valiantly to keep her mind on her work. But somehow her wayward thoughts kept slipping uncontrollably back to Eden Cassidy.

"I'm an experienced man. Why waste your time with a boy?''

The words, the whole repugnant scene, kept replaying in her head like a faulty videotape. Each time she felt the same mixture of emotions. Anger, abhorrence, repugnance. And a prurient excitement that horrified her.

Would she, could she ever forget those unthinkable words? His outrageous offer? She thought not.

The man was despicable, she told herself grimly as she made herself concentrate on the pile of work on her desk. He definitely wasn't worthy of the time she was wasting mulling over his outrageousness. She had a job to do and she wasn't going to allow the man to intrude on her thoughts any more than he already had.

She determinedly forced the scene from her mind and some time later, as she bent over a submission for their next issue, there was a tap on her office door, followed by the sound of the door opening.

"Keira—?'' Daniel began tentatively.

Keira didn't look up. "I said no interruptions, Daniel, and I meant it, so only three things will save you from a fate

worse than death. If you can see any blood. If the building's
on fire. Or if you're bearing hot coffee.''

"Having a hard day at the office, Mrs Strong?"

Keira's head snapped up and her startled grey eyes met
cold blue ones.

CHAPTER FIVE

"WHAT do you want?" The words were out before Keira could draw them back and the tone of her voice made her cringe at the audacity. "I mean, I'm pretty busy." She indicated the work on her desk and then sighed. "I'm sorry. I didn't mean to sound…" She paused, searching for a placating word that might defuse her previous brusqueness.

"Ungracious?" Eden Cassidy suggested with a quirk of his lips, lips that drew Keira's eyes without any conscious thought on her part.

Her heartbeats had began their now familiar dance and she swallowed quickly. She closed her mouth firmly as she went to apologise again.

Eden took a couple of steps into the room, stopping in front of her desk, and Daniel followed him, hovering awkwardly beside him, trying to convey to Keira a multitude of emotions in his expression. At any other time Keira would have been amused by Daniel's obvious mixture of bewilderment and reticence. However, at that moment she had other matters on her mind. And they all focused on the younger man's egotistical uncle.

What could he possibly want? Keira hadn't seen him since their altercation on the patio of the Cassidy mansion, hadn't thought ever to see him again.

She pushed herself to her feet, unwilling to give Eden Cassidy the advantage of towering over her. "If you've come to take Daniel to lunch then he's free to go, of course," she said, and Eden motioned her to return to her seat, lowering himself into the chair opposite her, setting his briefcase down on the floor beside him.

"I did have lunch in mind," he said easily. "But not with Daniel." His obvious meaning hung in the air between them as his gaze held hers, and Keira willed herself not to look away, refusing to acknowledge his enigmatic statement.

Lunch? With him? He had to be joking. But he was persistent, she'd give him that much. Although the reason for his apparent tenacity bothered her. Had his purported interest been further piqued by her reluctance to fall in with his impertinent plans to entice her into his bed?

Her mouth went suddenly dry at the thought. Silently she berated herself for her own lasciviousness and, contrary to the momentary racing of her senses, she refused to concede that the contemplation of such an erotic development excited her at all.

Casually she arched her eyebrows. "If you have some question concerning the magazine then I suggest you discuss it with Dianna," she began, and one corner of his mouth twisted derisively.

"I've just spent the last half-hour with Dianna doing just that, discussing the magazine," he put in abruptly. "I was simply asking you to have lunch with me," he finished evenly, narrowed eyes challenging her.

Keira's breathing fluctuated with her heartbeats and she made a show of shuffling some papers on her desk while she took an iron grip on her floundering composure. "I'm afraid I've got far too much work to do," she said, surprising herself with her firmness.

"You have to eat."

"We've had a few glitches this morning and I'm way behind. I'm just going to send out for a quick sandwich."

"You can have a sandwich if you like," he agreed easily. "But we'll get away from the office."

His dark brow rose as Keira's mouth opened slightly in disbelief.

Surely he didn't intend they should waste a couple of hours fighting their way through lunch-hour traffic to share a cosy meal at a fancy restaurant? Did he imagine she'd go with him, even if she could spare the time? Which she couldn't.

"And some coffee, wasn't it?" he added, challenging her again.

Keira spared a second to look at Daniel, who was regarding his uncle through narrowed eyes, obviously assessing this latest development. Then he noticed Keira's glance and changed his expression to one of bland interest.

"Why not have a decent lunch for once?" Daniel added his suggestion to his uncle's, and Eden's gaze centred momentarily on his nephew. "Wouldn't you prefer to go to a restaurant, Keira?" Daniel continued. "You're always grabbing a sandwich, and eating on the run is bad for your health, apart from the fact that the canteen serves cardboard food."

"You're exaggerating, Daniel," his uncle put in. "And for your information I didn't have the canteen in mind. We have a perfectly good restaurant in the building and I've made reservations for—" he glanced at his wristwatch "—five minutes' time. So shall we go, Keira?"

"I really can't..." Keira began, but Eden had turned back to his nephew.

"Don't let us keep you, Daniel. No doubt you've got work to do, too," Eden dismissed the younger man and Daniel's mouth tightened as a silent battle went on between the two men.

Keira saw the almost imperceptible jut of Daniel's chin as he flushed slightly. She had no wish to see Daniel embarrassed any further in a contest the younger man was ill-equipped to win.

"I'll no doubt see you before I leave," Eden added, and Daniel lifted his chin.

"Don't worry about that," he put in sulkily. "I'll be pretty busy and going from job to job so you probably won't catch up with me. I'll see you tonight at the apartment," he finished, a bite to his voice, and Eden glanced at him.

"I can only spare an hour," Keira cut in quickly and flashed Daniel what she hoped was a reassuring smile. "Perhaps you wouldn't mind letting Roxie know where I'll be if she needs me?"

Daniel hesitated for a moment, then gave Keira a meaningful look before nodding and leaving them, closing the door behind him with quiet hostility.

"Was it necessary to belittle Daniel in front of me?" Keira asked into the ensuing silence.

"You would have preferred I invite him to join us?" he came back coldly, his blue eyes chilling, and Keira snatched up her handbag.

"Not for the reasons you're implying. And if this is going to be another lecture of dire warnings about seducing your nephew then—"

"I have no intention of mentioning Daniel," he remarked drily. "I suspect it would only be giving you more ammunition to use against me. And I'm sure you have enough already," he added, his voice imperceptibly lower, a nuance that didn't pass unnoticed by Keira's sensitised nerve-endings.

"Shall we go?" He opened the door and stood back for Keira to precede him. "And perhaps we should stamp certain subjects taboo for the duration of the meal, in the interests of good digestion."

With one swift glance at the quirk of amusement that lifted the corners of his mouth, Keira stepped into the hallway.

If only he weren't so incredibly attractive to her. To every woman, she reminded herself caustically as she continued across to the lifts, every centimetre of her so aware of his hard body so close beside her. That he still had the power to move her more physical senses at a basic level shocked and to no small extent shamed her somehow.

She was a long way along from the virginal eighteen-year-old she'd been when she'd met Dennis, but she would hardly describe herself as a woman of the world in that respect.

Perhaps that was why her immediate response to this man, this so obviously experienced man, filled her with a fear of the hold his magnetism could exert over her. And the fear that her capitulation could be so overtly easy.

Fortunately the lift doors slid open immediately and Keira breathed a quick sigh of relief to see that at least half a dozen other people would be sharing the cubicle with them as they sped upwards.

The *maître d'* met them as they stepped into the restaurant, and it was obvious he had been waiting for Eden's arrival.

In no time at all they were seated at a table overlooking a magnificent panorama of the city and the harbour. As Keira watched, a Manly ferry left its berth by the Harbour Bridge and headed out to round the Opera House.

With a flourish the menus appeared and Keira gave hers her attention, trying to concentrate on the flowing script. But nothing seemed to make sense. Except the knowledge that Eden's body was so very close to hers. In fact she rather fancied she could feel the heat emanating from his skin. And if she moved her arm just a fraction they would touch.

She blinked, lifting her gaze over the top of the menu to meet Eden's steady blue eyes, and he raised his eyebrows enquiringly.

Keira realised he must have spoken and she moistened her dry lips with her tongue-tip. "I'm sorry. I'm not sure... I'm not really very hungry," she finished lamely and Eden reached across and took the menu from her nerveless fingers.

"Two club sandwiches," he said evenly as he handed the menus to the hovering waiter. "And some wine. My usual."

Keira drew a sharp breath, her eyes narrowing. She had to pull herself together, rebuild her resolve. Did he think he was going to woo her with expensive wine and an intimate setting?

And their table was secluded, she realised now. They were totally isolated from the other lunchers. Yes, it was far too intimate. And Eden Cassidy was far too close for comfort.

She had to put some distance between them. It was her only defence.

"What do you want, Mr Cassidy?" she repeated her earlier query as evenly as she could, deciding to return the ball firmly into his court.

"What do you think I want, Mrs Strong?" he countered, relaxing indolently back in his chair.

"I really can't imagine, but I suppose there is a reason why you came all the way down here. I mean, a man with a media conglomerate to run, one as extensive as Cassidy-Ford Publishing, wouldn't be visiting one of his lowly subsidiaries just to share an undoubtedly expensive club sandwich with..." She paused, valiantly trying to finish the sentence without becoming even more enmeshed in the conversational web she'd woven about herself.

"With?" he prompted, infuriatingly nonchalant, but Keira's mind had drawn a blank. "With a very attractive woman?" he suggested, and her hackles rose, but only after she'd consciously quelled that split second of heady excitement his provocative words evoked.

"With one of your insignificant underlings," she bit out, her grey eyes bright with an anger that was aimed as much at herself as it was at him. "Especially one who has so recently knocked you back," she added, unable to guard her impetuous tongue.

"Knocked me back?" He shook his dark head in mock dismay. "Come now, Keira, I prefer to refer to it as exercised your freedom of choice. Much more refined, don't you think?"

Keira watched him sceptically. Was his seemingly genuine bonhomie another ploy? Or had his ego taken her rejection of his outrageous proposal without offence? In the unlikely event that this was so, then why *was* he here?

One fairly obvious reason came immediately to mind. The rumours that had been rife throughout the magazine's staff in the past week, rumours of employment cuts.

Keira went a little cold. Was he going to fire her? Wine her and dine her and then tell her he was dispensing with her services? That her failure to take him up on his blatant proposition was to put paid to her career?

If that was the case, he'd find he'd victimised the wrong woman. She'd never allow him to get away with it. She'd...

"Wrong on all counts, Keira," he said seriously, straightening in his chair as the waiter appeared with the wine. They spent several moments while a taste was proffered to Eden and he'd nodded an acknowledgment.

"As a matter of fact I have come to discuss business. And this time I think I'll have an offer you can't refuse," he added, his lips twisting self-derisively as he raised his glass to his lips.

Keira watched, that same traitorous craving rising in her, until she was almost hypnotised by the pursing of his lips on the wine glass, the movement of the muscles in his throat as he swallowed, and she had to force herself to concentrate on his words. Desperately she took a gulp of her own wine.

"However, before we go into that," he was continuing, "I'd like you to tell me something about *Natural Life*."

Keira sat forward in surprise. "With respect to what? Cassidy-Ford bought the magazine over five years ago and—'' she shrugged ''—a couple of issues later it was discontinued.''

''You started the magazine with a friend, I believe.''

''Yes. With a schoolfriend. We were cadet journalists together and we decided to try *Natural Life* on a small scale and see how it went. We were reasonably successful considering the fact that we were novices and produced the whole thing on a shoestring budget. We were just beginning to get our heads above water financially when Cassidy-Ford made its offer. But you must know all this.'' Keira set down her glass and absently rubbed at the tension in the back of her neck.

''Why did you sell out?'' he asked without comment.

''Why wouldn't we, when the price was right?'' Keira parried.

''Humour me with this, Keira, hmm?'' he said equitably, his voice quietly persuasive. ''What was the real reason?'' he persisted, and Keira sighed, knowing she had no defence against his pervasive probing.

''Gail, my partner, married a few months before I did but within the year she'd given birth to a set of twins, so she was finding it difficult to devote as much time to the magazine as it required. She felt bad about putting more and more of the physical burden on me so—'' Keira gestured resignedly with her hands ''—we decided the best interests of the magazine and our small staff would be served by accepting your offer. Gail and I both got our financial investment back and none of the staff, including myself, lost jobs.''

''Why do you think Cassidy-Ford discontinued the publishing of the magazine? It was a growing concern when we bought it. What went wrong?''

Keira eyed him undecidedly and took another stalling sip of her wine, suddenly becoming aware that she'd almost finished her glass.

''Don't get evasive on me,'' he said quickly. ''You've

been honest, sometimes brutally so, until now, and I can assure you I wouldn't ask if I didn't want your opinion."

"Fair enough. I think you had too many overheads for the limited market. We were producing the number of magazines to fill the demand. When Cassidy-Ford took over they tried to increase that demand when the demand wasn't there." Keira regarded him levelly. "Of course, I could be wrong."

Eden's lips quirked but he made no comment as the waiter materialised with their meal. He placed before them an appetising stack of sandwiches surrounded by crisp salad, and only when she looked at the well-presented food did Keira realise she *was* hungry. Her tummy tightened as she reached for her cutlery.

They ate in silence for some time and only when Keira set down her fork did Eden motion to the waiter for coffee.

"Now, where were we?" he remarked when they were alone again. "Ah, yes. You were telling me where we went wrong with *Natural Life*."

"You did ask for my opinion," Keira put in quickly. "And that's simply what I gave you. My opinion."

Eden took a sip of his coffee, grimaced, and added a little more sugar. "Don't be so prickly. Although I suppose you have every right to be, don't you? Look, Keira, perhaps we started out on the wrong foot. Well, I did, anyway. But I'd prefer not to be in constant dispute with you."

"I really can't see any point in—" Keira started to say, and he held up his hand.

"Hear me out, Keira, before you give me the verbal reprimand I undoubtedly deserve. I've spoken to Daniel and he assures me you are just good friends."

"Which I also told you," Keira put in drily.

"Which you also told me," he agreed easily. "However, in my defence, as Daniel's guardian I was simply concerned about him. We haven't been seeing eye to eye lately over this business about deferring his studies so—" he shrugged

"—I guess I was all primed up to over-react and I did. I'd like to apologise. So let's call a truce, hmm?"

Keira held his dark gaze for long moments before giving a slight acquiescing nod, while her defences suggested vehemently that she keep up her guard.

"All that aside, I wanted to say I know just how good you are at your job," Eden continued evenly. "And I'm aware of how much of yourself you put into *Chloe*. It shows in the finished product."

"I'm just the assistant editor, Mr Cassidy." Keira fought the wave of pleasure that washed over her at his praise. Yet part of her warned her to beware. "Dianna—"

"For God's sake, call me Eden," he broke in. "And I don't want to discuss Dianna Forester. Can't you accept a compliment on your ability for what it's worth?"

"When there aren't any strings attached, yes, I can," Keira replied just as forthrightly, and Eden sighed exasperatedly.

"I thought we'd finished with that. There aren't any strings, I assure you. Now, to get back to *Natural Life*. If we decided to recommence publication, what would you like to see retained, discarded or added?"

"Are you going to publish the magazine again?"

"Perhaps. Our research shows that today's climate is more suitable for that type of publication."

"How long have you been considering reissuing *Natural Life*?" Keira asked him suspiciously, wondering if he might have conjured up what may very well be a bogus ploy to do more checking on a woman he considered an unacceptable match for his nephew.

Eden shrugged. "A couple of months. We've done all the research and now I'm here to confer with you as the magazine's previous editor," he finished blandly. "So, let's hear your ideas."

His query seemed genuine enough, Keira thought uneasily and then she frowned, realising that in spite of her misgivings he'd peaked her interest. "If you intend to pick up where you left off with *Natural Life* then I think perhaps you need to broaden its guidelines. Don't aim the magazine at one socio-economic group. The articles should be of interest to a more diverse audience than they were before. The focus of the original magazine was fairly limited."

Eden opened his briefcase and took out a folder, shifting his coffee-cup so he could spread it out in front of him. "I have a list of the regular features, those which rated highly and those our survey suggested we discard."

He handed Keira a loose sheet and she glanced down at it, skimming the list with interest before she nodded and went to pass the paper back to him.

"Keep it. I have my copy here. Do you think the survey was on track?" he asked.

"Pretty much so. I agree the articles should appeal to both sexes. With both men and women working, the woman isn't necessarily the exclusive homemaker, even more so now than was the case ten years ago. There should also be something geared to the unemployed, of interest but still affordable."

Eden made short, concise notes on his copy and Keira watched the sure movements of his hand, the furrow of complete attention etched between his dark brows. And the unnerving part of her that registered his undeniable physical attributes swung so easily into gear that she tensed painfully. Her nerve endings quivered, the sensations all but distracting her, and she had to force herself to regain her own concentration.

"Nowadays a lot more people are interested in the environment," she continued quickly, "so I feel a magazine like this one could carry more information about that, especially articles that are plain and easy to understand, targeted at the layman and not bogged down in a lot of technical mumbo jumbo."

Eden smiled faintly and Keira flushed, but persisted defiantly.

"I'd also like to see occasional reports on the national heritage, exclusively Australian. That was something we planned before we sold the magazine. As a matter of fact you could probably use and expand a lot of the by-lines from the old magazine," she added thoughtfully.

"Such as?" he enquired, looking up.

"Well, perhaps the general everyday information columns."

Eden consulted his notes again. "I see one of your most popular and successful columns was a write-in question-answer type on health, naturopathy, pets, etcetera, called 'Ask Aunt Aggie'."

"Yes," Keira agreed slowly, "It featured household hints, repairs and remedies, and old-fashioned recipes using tried and true methods which struck a happy medium between ones that are quick and easy using natural ingredients, and ones that began with 'go out and slaughter your ox'. Of course, the name's a little trite but—" she shrugged "—it worked."

Eden sat back regarding her and Keira shifted uneasily in her seat. "We got good feedback on that particular column," he said thoughtfully. "So, you feel the magazine would work this time around?"

Keira nodded. "I don't see why it wouldn't. Allowing that this isn't the best economic climate for starting a business venture, the magazine would have to have topical appeal and if your research points out that it does, well, it sounds more than viable."

Eden consulted his file. "And some of these contributors—do you think they would be available to work on *Natural Life* again? Especially this Miss Agatha Rains, who apparently created Ask Aunt Aggie?"

A small smile played about Keira's lips and Eden's eyes narrowed to centre on them. "There'd be no problem with

Aunt Aggie, and I'm sure the others would also be available.''

"Good. Which brings me to my final question. How would you like to take on the job of editor of the revamped *Natural Life*?"

Keira stared at him for surprised seconds. "Me? But—"

"You've done it before."

"Not on the scale you're obviously talking about and, besides, we're snowed under at the moment. I couldn't spare the time from *Chloe* right now."

"I wouldn't expect you to cover both positions. As I said, you've been doing an outstanding job."

Keira went to speak and Eden held up his hand. "And I know all about the situation that exists with the staff. I've been aware of it for some time. Let's leave it at that and not go into the politics of personalities, hmm? I wouldn't offer you this promotion if I didn't think you could handle it. All that remains is for you to decide whether or not you want it."

"I'm flattered but I... Well, I haven't really given any thought to changing jobs. I expected to..."

"Go on doing what you're doing now? One of my snoops—" he grimaced "—tells me you can do the job with your eyes closed. That's no challenge."

Keira felt her cheeks colour. "What makes you think I need a challenge?" she asked shakily, and he raised one dark brow.

"Let's just say I'm a fantastic judge of character. So, yes or no?"

"You want to know right now?"

"Why not now?"

"There are considerations. I mean, what happens with *Chloe*?"

"All that will be taken care of."

"And what about staff for the new magazine?"

"You can choose your own staff." He removed another

sheet from his folder and passed it across to her. "That's a suggested list of positions. Read it through and you can make your recommendations to fill them. You can create or delete if you feel it's necessary and we'll discuss it."

Keira glanced down at the list in amazement. On paper it seemed as though she could write her own ticket, so to speak. It was far too good to be true. Would she have to pay for such generosity in the long run, be held on a tight editorial rein by the powers-that-be?

"If I do take the position I'd want to know what or who I'll be up against," she said slowly, and Eden Cassidy provocatively held her gaze.

"Who you'll be up against? Now there's a thought," he said softly, and Keira's heartbeats accelerated in immediate response.

"You wish," she said as softly, smiling despite herself, and he raised one fine dark brow again.

"Oh, I do. I can't dispute that. However, that has nothing whatsoever to do with *Natural Life* and I wouldn't be foolish enough to jeopardise Cassidy-Ford's chances of getting the best person for this position. So I'd better reassure you I'd only be on the periphery of the venture. Technically, you'd be top dog. And you needn't even contact me directly if you didn't want to. You could report via Denver Clarkson, as Dianna does now."

"And I'd have final say as to my staff?"

He nodded.

"You say I'd have editorial independence but just what would that mean in terms of the day-to-day editorial decisions?"

"It would be exactly the same as it is with *Chloe*. I have trust in you and your judgement. You've edited this type of magazine before and you've excelled in your present position. I see no problem with your having editorial autonomy."

Keira returned her gaze to the papers in front of her.

Tremors of excitement welled within her. It was really the job she'd been working towards all these years since the failure of her marriage. Admittedly she'd allowed her ambition to slip on to the back burner this past year or so, but there was no denying that a position such as the one he was offering her had been her goal, the pinnacle of her chosen career.

Now it was within her grasp. She simply had to reach out and take it. And less than a week ago she would have killed for this chance.

So why was she hesitating? Her heart skipped a beat. The answer to that question sat right in front of her. Climbing this rung of the ladder took her one step closer to Eden Cassidy.

She was well aware that Dianna Forester, as editor of one of Cassidy-Ford's publications, often attended various meetings where Eden Cassidy presided. Dianna would return and with studied casualness drop his name into the conversation, much to Roxie Denahey's disgust.

Keira's mind shot off at another tangent. Roxie would be the first person she'd add to her new staff. Roxie was competent and trustworthy and they got on so well, always had, which wasn't the case with Roxie and Dianna.

She could also offer positions to— Keira stopped the direction of her train of thought. She was acting as though she'd decided to take on the job when...

"What's your decision?" Eden's deep voice made her start slightly and she raised grey eyes to meet his. "Assistant editor of the tried and true, or editor of our new endeavour?"

CHAPTER SIX

DANIEL knocked tentatively and entered Keira's office. "I just saw Eden leaving. So how was lunch?"

"Fine." Keira shrugged non-committally.

"Eden *has* gone, hasn't he?" Daniel said. "Or is he likely to turn up again?"

"He's gone as far as I know," Keira said without intonation, feeling as though she'd been through an emotional wringer and not sure she wasn't still trapped in one. "You just missed him."

"Good."

Keira sighed. "Look, Daniel, if this is going to be long and involved I haven't got the time to listen and commiserate, so could you be brief or preferably save it for tomorrow?"

"Did he rub you up the wrong way again?" asked Daniel sympathetically, and Keira frowned.

"No. Not that it's any of your business, but your uncle didn't rub me the wrong way. I simply have stacks of work to get through. A point I've been fruitlessly trying to make all day."

"Cat was here," Daniel said with high drama. "I've told her all about you and I wanted her to meet you. You see, we'd arranged to have lunch today and then Eden turned up just when I was expecting Cat. I nearly had a heart attack."

"If you brought it all out in the open you wouldn't have to sneak about," Keira told him tiredly. "You should have taken the opportunity to introduce them."

"Not likely. But at least once I knew Eden was in the building I knew where he'd be."

Keira raised her eyebrows.

"Well, if he was in the building and you were in the same building then I reckon it would be a fair bet that he would be somewhere near you."

Keira was unable to prevent warm colour flooding her cheeks. "You're being ridiculous," she stated, and made a slash on the page with her red pen.

"Not as I see it. The penny dropped a while ago when I was watching you two together. So, what happened between you and Eden at the weekend?"

"What makes you think anything happened?" Keira asked without looking up.

"The fact that you're both trying to pretend nothing happened. I only mentioned you at dinner last night and Eden nearly snapped my head off. This morning I said something about Eden to you and you were almost as bad." Daniel sat down, looking seriously into Keira's eyes. "Eden didn't make a pass at you, did he? When I left you alone with him on the patio? You seemed a little distracted after that."

Keira felt her flush deepen. "Daniel! Enough already! I was tired, that's all."

"Ahh!" Daniel nodded knowingly.

"Ahh nothing." Keira looked pointedly at her wrist-watch. "It's after five. I hope you won't have the nerve to claim overtime."

"Overtime? I'm deeply offended. You know I'm not a clock-watcher, Keira."

"No. You're a real little trouper, Daniel. Now, would you please buzz off and let me get on with my work?"

"OK. I understand you don't want to talk about it but I kind of feel responsible, you know. If I hadn't talked you into going with me at the weekend—"

"Daniel," Keira appealed, and he stood up.

"All right. I can take a hint. But I think I should sort of—you know, warn you."

"Warn me?" Keira gazed at him levelly. "Warn me about what?"

"Well, about Eden. Over the years he's had more than his share of women." Daniel grimaced. "But none of them have lasted for long. Except for Megan, I guess," he added with a frown. "But you're different, Keira. I just wouldn't want you to get hurt."

Keira drew herself up in her chair, ignoring the pain inside that told her she knew what Daniel was saying was true. "I've no intention of getting involved with your uncle," she said through clenched teeth, and Daniel had the grace to look a little disconcerted.

"I just wanted to say there've been plenty of women in his past."

"Everyone has a past, Daniel."

"I know. But earlier I thought you and Eden were—you know, aware of each other."

"Your imagination must have been in overdrive." Keira made a show of shuffling the pages in front of her.

"Well, you have to admit he's good-looking. And he's rich. Women drop like flies around him."

"Charming, Daniel. You have a way with words."

"You know what I mean, Keira."

"All I know is that a moment ago you were warning me off and now you're singing his praises."

"I have this theory that maybe all he needs is a good woman to save him from himself, or whatever it is good women save a man from," he added with a grin.

"I'll let that remark pass, only because I sense a deliberate provocation."

"So why not you and Eden, Keira? Seriously. I think you'd be great together."

"Daniel—" Keira glared at him and he backed off a few paces.

"OK, I know. Subject closed. So I'll see you tomorrow."

You and Eden. Keira shook her head quickly as Daniel left her. It was pointless weighing up the pros and cons of a prospective relationship with Eden Cassidy. She knew exactly what it would involve. A physical fling, undoubtedly exciting, and then the uncertainty as he cooled off before the painful parting when he tired of her. No, if she'd needed any reminding then one of Daniel's comments had jogged her memory.

Eden Cassidy had had a lot of women. And Keira wasn't going to add herself to the list. She wasn't interested in just an affair.

Apart from that, he was her boss, a boss who'd just offered her the job of a lifetime. And as she'd accepted the position she had no intention of jeopardising it in any way. Especially by becoming involved with the head of Cassidy-Ford Publishing.

To do that she'd have to be out of her mind. And the last thing she needed was complications in her private life, earth-shatteringly exciting complications though they might be. Right now she would need to focus all her attention on making the magazine's resurrection a success.

And as attractive as Eden Cassidy undoubtedly was, well... Keira sighed and passed her hand tiredly over her eyes. Attractive? He was the most magnetic man she'd ever met and she couldn't deny she was physically aware of him, that the feelings he stirred within her she'd never felt quite so strongly before. The fact remained that he would always be out of her league. She'd just have to keep reminding herself of that.

Unable to prevent herself, Keira picked up the job structure list Eden had left with her and she began pencilling in some suggestions. Glancing at the time, she shook her head and began to tidy her desk. She knew she'd never get any more work done this evening so she might as well go home, begin early in the morning when she was fresh and, hopefully, had regained her concentration.

It took a full two days for word about the new magazine and Keira's promotion to become common knowledge around the office.

However, at least Keira had been able to discuss it with her editor before the rumors began. Dianna had sought Keira out and they'd talked about the upheaval of Keira's subsequent replacement and how it would affect *Chloe*. Although the meeting hadn't been overly painful, that Dianna was not pleased about the changes was obvious.

This morning Eden and Denver Clarkson were coming to see Keira to discuss some of the more pressing arrangements regarding the staffing of the new venture.

When a knock sounded on the door Keira took a steadying breath before responding. Daniel strode purposefully over to the desk and leaned across to take Keira's hand.

"Take me with you, Keira," he beseeched earnestly. "You know I'd do anything for you, I'll work like a slave. Anything."

"For heaven's sake, Daniel. Don't you know that walls have ears? You don't know who could be listening."

"Everyone knows Eden's due to arrive so they're all at their various desks making industrious working noises."

"Yes, well, let's just say I'm over-sensitive. I've suffered more than enough repercussions since that party I should never have let you talk me into attending. And trying to explain why I went with you..." Keira expelled an expressive breath and Daniel laughed.

"It was the good old Cassidy charm."

Keira pulled a face at him and he grinned delightedly.

"Anyway, so what do you say?"

"About what exactly?"

"About the new magazine. Can I work with you on *Nat-*

ural Life? You said you were pleased with my work, that I showed promise.''

''I am and you do,'' Keira acknowledged shortly. ''But I thought you liked it here on *Chloe*?''

''I do, but I want to stay on your team.''

Keira regarded him thoughtfully.

''Want me to go down on bended knee and beg?'' Daniel made to carry out his threat and Keira held up her hand.

''Don't you dare, Daniel Cassidy. There's no need for any theatricals. And before you waste any more of my time, I've already decided to have you with us.''

''You have? That's great.'' Daniel beamed. ''Can't live without me, huh?''

''You're pushing your luck,'' Keira replied wryly. ''Now, we've both got work to do. How about showing me what a willing slave you are instead of talking about it? And close the door as you leave.''

''For you, boss lady, I'd climb the highest mountain. Walk across the desert.'' He turned and gave her a salute. ''And swim the deepest ocean,'' he added with a laugh, closing the door before Keira could retaliate.

The door opened again almost immediately and, an easy smile still lifting the corners of her mouth, Keira looked up, expecting to see Daniel again, but in his place stood a tall, now familiar figure filling the doorway.

''Do you elicit such great loyalty from all your staff or is it just peculiar to the Cassidys?'' Eden asked softly as he leant one broad shoulder against the door-jamb.

''Your nephew has a strange sense of humour,'' Keira replied, his sudden appearance setting her thoughts scattering like leaves in an autumn wind.

''So it would seem,'' Eden said caustically, and straightened. ''And it appears he spends a considerable amount of his day in your office.''

Keira lifted her chin. ''No more than anyone else does,'' she stated firmly, and Eden's lips thinned.

"From memory, he's been here every time I have."

"And he usually has a valid reason for being here. He does work on this magazine, you know."

"But he's not supposed to be working exclusively for you."

"He doesn't," Keira bit back, and he gave an exclamation of disbelief.

"Anyone would think—"

"No," Keira broke in on him. "Anyone wouldn't. Only you seem to read evil intentions into it when there's really nothing there. Unless there's something about Daniel I don't know."

"What are you talking about?" he demanded tersely.

"Well, you must have some reason for your unfounded suspicions. Does Daniel make a habit of pursuing older women?"

He eyed her coldly. "Not until now," he said levelly.

"And, as I've told you before, he still isn't. Look, can we leave this? I'm beginning to find the whole subject distasteful and if you persist in bringing it up every time we meet then I'll begin to suspect there's something else behind it all."

"Like what?" he snapped, and Keira shrugged.

"How about plain out-and-out jealousy?" she suggested, surprising herself with her frankness.

"Jealousy?" he repeated ominously. "Are you implying—?" He bit off an expletive and his lips compressed. "I am not jealous of my nephew."

"And I'm not so sex-starved that I'd be driven to chasing a teenage boy to engage in what, in my opinion, is a highly over-rated activity."

As the words came out of her mouth Keira wished she could draw them back inside. But before Eden could make what Keira expected would be a disparaging comment there was the sound of footsteps in the hallway and he turned slightly.

"Morning, Denver. Come on in." Eden stood aside for the other man, his expression now devoid of its previous displeasure. "You know Mrs Strong, of course."

Denver Clarkson was a slightly built man on the wrong side of fifty, his sandy hair thinning on his head. Although Keira had been aware of him since she had joined the staff of *Chloe*, she had rarely come into contact with him. His dealings had usually been with Dianna. Now he pushed his steel-framed glasses up his sharp nose and held out his hand.

"Nice to see you, Mrs Strong. I believe congratulations are in order."

"Thank you." Keira had regained some of her composure and managed to smile at him before motioning for the two men to sit down.

"All your diligent work has paid off," Denver commented easily enough as he seated himself, but Keira felt a small sense of disquiet in the pit of her stomach.

"I suppose it has," she replied reluctantly, wondering if she was imagining the almost imperceptible disapproval in his light tone, in his ingratiating smile.

"We've had our eye on Keira for some time," Eden put in, and Keira did not miss the sudden pursing of Denver Clarkson's lips when Eden used her Christian name.

"Yes, she's always shown promise," Denver agreed affably enough. "Well done, my dear."

For the next couple of hours they discussed various aspects and policies of the new magazine and by the time the two men stood to leave Keira's head was spinning. But she had to admit she hadn't felt so elated in ages. She really was looking forward to this new project, and the faint feelings of lethargy she'd been experiencing of late had totally disappeared.

Setting aside her notes, she stood up, moving around her desk to see the two men to the door.

"Congratulations again, Mrs Strong, and good luck with this new enterprise." Denver held out his hand again. "No doubt we'll be interacting far more often in the future. I'm sure we're going to get along just fine.''

"Thank you. I'm looking forward to it," Keira said politely, suspecting Denver Clarkson was thinking nothing of the kind. She hoped he wasn't going to be the drawback in this otherwise ideal opportunity.

Denver looked at his watch. "I have a progress meeting with some of the union reps in ten minutes." He pulled a face. "Perhaps you'd like to come along, Eden, try to talk some sense into a couple of the young hotheads. I think Doug Craigie and I would both appreciate it."

"Sure. You go along, Denver. I'll join you presently. I have a couple more things to discuss with Keira."

"Of course." Denver smiled, his pale eyes going from his boss to Keira before he left them, closing the door quietly behind him.

What could Eden be thinking about, singling her out like this? Keira coloured in embarrassment. Couldn't he see the speculation in the other man's eyes? Now he was only adding fuel to what was obviously Denver Clarkson's misconception about their relationship.

Was that what everyone in the corporation would think when they heard, what those who knew were already thinking? Perhaps this was the real reason for Dianna Forester's coolness towards her. Because Keira now realised she hadn't misinterpreted Denver's earlier veiled disapproval of her. Denver and Dianna, and who knew how many others, thought she'd slept her way into the job.

Keira almost groaned. And Eden Cassidy wasn't helping the situation.

Agitatedly she walked across and opened the door Denver had closed. "I really don't want to keep you from the meeting," she began in a rush as Eden's cool gaze went pointedly to the door she still held open.

Silently he reached out and just as casually closed the

door again, bringing another rush of embarrassed colour to Keira's cheeks.

"What's the problem, Keira?" he asked, his level gaze holding hers.

"I...I know you must be busy and I thought...Mr Clarkson said... The meeting sounds important," she finished quickly and took a deep breath, valiantly trying to steady her now racing heartbeat. Eden must know what was going on. How could he help knowing?

"Denver's handled countless similar negotiations on his own before." Eden relaxed back against the now closed door, one hand in the pocket of his grey trousers, his suit coat open to reveal the tailored matching waistcoat that hugged his broad chest. "I'm in no hurry."

Keira's eyes slid quickly over him, her flush heating her already warm face as a small smile played around the corners of his sensual mouth. She straightened, drawing herself together. There was obviously no point in beating about the bush. "I just don't think this is a good idea, that's all. You must see that," she added in a rush.

"I'm afraid I don't see. Perhaps you should be more explicit, hmm?"

"Closing the door. Staying here to talk to me alone," Keira got out tensely.

"Why shouldn't I?"

"People might... People will think..." Her voice gave out on her.

"Will think?" he prompted.

"That... Oh, don't be obtuse. Don't pretend you don't know what I'm talking about. You must realise what they're thinking. It was written all over Denver Clarkson's face."

Eden raised dark brows, infuriating Keira even more.

She turned, took a couple of paces away from him, her fingers agitatedly twisting the dress ring on her right hand. "You know they're thinking I landed this job via the casting couch."

"And you know you didn't," he remarked easily.

Keira swung back to face him, her grey eyes flashing angrily. "Yes, well, that's the only good thing about this—this fiasco."

"It's going to be rather difficult to tell everyone you turned me down," he said, the flash of humour in his eyes belying the seriousness of his expression. "But if you'd like I can give it a try. However, it may seem like a smokescreen, a case of protesting too much, methinks."

"Oh, for heaven's sake! You may find this hilarious but I can assure you it isn't a joke to me, Mr Cassidy." Keira lifted her chin. "I'm a private person and I rather value my reputation, both personally and professionally. Now if that's something someone like you finds it difficult to understand, then I'm sorry, but I have to work with these people."

"I think you're over-reacting," he said calmly. "Those who know you won't believe it and, as I said before, you know the truth. And so do I," he added with a casual shrug.

"Unfortunately that doesn't do much in the eyes of the gossips. Especially when you act as perfunctorily, as irresponsibly, as you just did."

A frown furrowed his brow as he straightened and she sensed he had tensed imperceptibly. "I really can't see how closing an office door compromises your reputation."

"Closing it the way you did in front of Denver Clarkson was hardly prudent under the circumstances," she stated with a wave of her hand.

"Good lord, this isn't the Victorian era. We're both single and adults." Eden faced her, hands aggressively on his hips now. "And I hardly think Denver Clarkson gives a damn what we do behind closed doors."

"Well, I do give a damn."

"Look, Keira," he appealed, reaching out to clasp her arm, and Keira started away from him.

His head went up then, his eyes darkening as his own anger surged to equal hers. In one fluid stride he'd followed her, his fingers finding and encircling her wrist, and she found herself propelled against the solid wall of his chest.

Her eyes widened in astonished alarm for short seconds, and then a far more potent emotion surged from deep within her. Suddenly every erotic response in her body found life, stood at full alert, the shock of the intensity of her awareness rendering her completely paralysed.

Part of her mind urgently told her to thrust him away from her, put a steadying distance between them. Yet most of her, those horrifyingly unprecedented feelings of sensual desire, craved for her surrender. Electrifying emotions seared through her to explode at every sensitised nerve ending, clamouring for her to match anything he cared to offer.

His own anger had diminished too. She recognised that same incendiary hunger in his darkened eyes, for it was like looking into the mirror of her own soul. And she knew without reservation that he wanted her just as much as she wanted him.

CHAPTER SEVEN

A THICKLY sensual sound broke from his throat and his head descended with a slowness that for Keira was very nearly an agony of waiting. His eyes never wavered from hers, each torturous moment holding a so temptingly seductive promise.

Her mouth was suddenly aflame, awaiting the touch of his, and her throat constricted achingly as her heartbeats reverberated in her breast.

Keira's chin lifted of its own accord and when their lips finally met she heard a thunderous rushing in her ears and felt as though she were drowning, swirling downwards in a vortex of pleasure and pain.

They kissed for minutes, or hours, both oblivious to the passing of time, tongue-tips touching, plundering, exciting each other in a torrent of delirious intensity.

Somehow Eden had turned them around, his hips now resting against her desk. One taut thigh insinuated itself tantalisingly between hers and his hand slid slowly down her back to hold her firmly against him.

Keira's bones seemed to melt and the fire in the pit of her stomach exploded into an inferno. She moaned softly, moving sensually against him and he pulled her impossibly closer, his lips sliding feverishly along the line of her jaw, the curve of her throat, to settle in the V where the neckline of her blouse skimmed the swell of her breasts.

He drew her blouse from her skirt, his hand slipping over her smooth midriff to cup her breast through the lace of her bra, and when his fingers found her straining nipple her knees gave way beneath her. Keira let herself collapse against him, and she knew she was just as aroused as he so obviously was. She rained light, passionate kisses over his face, the tip of her tongue teasing his earlobe as his fingers on her breast drove her to the brink of ecstatic desire.

And that she was almost past the point of no return some small far-off part of her realised, tried to warn her, and she groaned at the intrusive thought. She didn't want to think. Or to rationalise her revealing response.

With eyes closed she threw her head back invitingly and his lips trailed smouldering fire over her throat. Then she opened her eyes, her smoky gaze locking with his, and somehow the earth shifted slightly off its axis before righting itself and bringing them just marginally back into kilter.

For long soul-searching moments they gazed at each other, both hovering on the high of their arousal, and it was Eden who broke the heady, electrified silence.

''Perhaps we'd better lock that damn door,'' he said huskily, his blue eyes still dark liquid pools of molten desire.

Keira blinked languidly, only slowly beginning to take in the picture they made.

Somehow her fingers had fumblingly undone his waistcoat, slid between the buttons of his shirt to settle in the mat of fine hair on his chest. The skirt of her suit was high on her thighs, displaying her nylon-clad legs, and his hand still rested on her swollen breast beneath her blouse.

If anyone walked in and saw them now...

Keira drew back as though she had been stung. Or attempted to. For at her withdrawal Eden's arm about her had tightened and she struggled, her hands pushing against the hard wall of his chest.

''Let me go!'' she demanded, her voice catching in her throat. ''Eden, please! This is madness—''

''Divine madness,'' he said softly, and held her fast for long moments before he finally slowly released her.

Keira agitatedly pulled down her skirt and began to straighten her blouse, her fingers shaking as she tucked it into her belt. "For God's sake, fix your shirt. Anyone could come in and..."

"And they'd be suitably shocked, I'm sure," he finished drily as he pushed himself to his feet and buttoned his waistcoat. "Very short-sighted of us. It would seem our emotions got the better of us, hmm?"

Keira ran a hand over her eyes. "I can't believe..." She shook her head, completely mortified by her behaviour. "This can't be happening..."

Realising she was babbling, she took a steadying breath. "How could you—?" She heard what she was saying and stopped.

No. In all fairness she couldn't totally blame Eden. She was just as culpable as he was for their disgusting display of abandonment.

Keira fought to regain her composure. "I'm sorry. I didn't mean to imply that this—" she swallowed painfully "—that this was all your fault," she finished with as much dignity as she could muster.

"Thank you. That's very charitable of you," he replied with equal aplomb, and she glanced at him sharply.

"There's no need to be condescending," she retorted. "I fully accept part of the responsibility. I simply don't know quite what possessed me to act—well, the way I did."

"I told you it was inevitable, Keira," he said evenly and she glared at him, her eyes flashing.

"Is that all you can say? Well, that's your opinion. I happen to disagree. I wouldn't have said it was inevitable and—" she gulped a breath, trying to ignore the vivid memories of the two of them on the dance floor at Sir Samuel's party "—and I'd like you to...I think it would be best if we try to forget it ever happened."

"In *your* opinion, hmm? But can you forget, Keira?" His

deep voice flowed over her, rekindling embers that still glowed within her.

"Yes. Yes, I can," she said, again with more conviction than she felt. "If we both agree not to mention it then I think we should be able to put it behind us and, well, just go on from here."

"As though nothing happened?" he repeated without intonation.

Keira lifted her chin. "Yes."

He was silent for long, oppressive moments and then he gave an abruptly sceptical laugh. "I'm afraid I don't think I can do that."

"What...what do you mean?" Keira got out through suddenly dry lips, and Eden shrugged.

"I mean I don't care to forget it ever happened."

A multitude of outrageously unconscionable thoughts skittered about inside Keira's mind, not the least being the surge of renewed excitement that perhaps he found her desirable enough to... She pulled herself together with no little effort.

"A moment longer and we'd have been right there on the floor making love," he continued harshly.

"Making love?" She gave a bitter laugh. "You're being generous. I'd hardly call it that."

"Making love. Having sex. No matter what name you give it, we would have been doing it. Can you honestly deny that, Keira?" he demanded, and she paced over to her desk, shaking her head exasperatedly before swinging back to face him.

"Perhaps not," she agreed with distaste. "But we can only be thankful we came to our senses before we did something I can assure you I'd have regretted even more. So—" Keira made herself hold his stormy gaze "—I'm afraid you'll have to try to forget it. Because I don't intend to have an affair with my boss and feed the avaricious appetite of the trouble-making gossipmongers."

His eyes continued to sear into hers for long seconds before his lashes fell to shield his expression. "Very forceful words, my dear," he remarked wearily, as though the subject suddenly bored him, and he crossed to the door, pulling it open before he turned back to face her.

"By the way, unbelievable as it may now seem, I did legitimately want to discuss something with you. You'll be needing new office space for *Natural Life* and a floor has just become available in one of our buildings three streets south of here. You'll be moving in there almost immediately and you'll operate from the twelfth floor. In Cassidy-Ford Towers."

The corner of his mouth quirked sardonically. "My offices are in the same building, so it looks as if there'll be more food for your gossips, Keira," he added as he turned and left her.

For the next six weeks Keira worked harder than she had for years. There was the handing over of her job on *Chloe* to her successor and the move to their new offices. Although most of the groundwork had been done for the revamped magazine there were new staff to be hired, contributors to be contacted, interviews to be set up and coordinated and a hundred and one details to be seen to that kept them all on the hop.

Gail, Keira's ex-partner, was overjoyed at the chance to contribute to the magazine again. Her twins were now in pre-school so she had some time on her hands and the part-time work suited her down to the ground.

Keira also dug out her late aunt's recipe books and diaries to recommence the Ask Aunt Aggie column which had been so popular in the old magazine. She hadn't told Eden that she had been responsible for that by-line. Keira's Aunt Aggie had been meticulous in recording her favourite recipes and effective old-fashioned remedies.

Of course, the mere thought of working in Cassidy-Ford

Towers had filled her with a mixture of apprehensive excitement and abject trepidation. She seemed to be continu-
ously keyed up in the expectation of meeting Eden in the
building.

Even though she kept reminding herself that an executive,
in this case the top executive, with exclusive offices on the
top floor, one floor below his penthouse apartment, would
not be likely to use the ordinary bank of lifts. He would
have his own express lift.

Yet Keira still entered the building each morning with
agitated anticipation, her eyes hastily scanning the foyer for
that familiar tall, dark, suit-clad figure.

However, after the first couple of weeks passed un-
eventfully she began to relax a little. And she even pre-
tended she'd convinced herself that the unbelievably erotic
episode in her old office had been just a figment of one very
base facet of her imagination.

Yes, she'd almost convinced herself of that. Her body's
responses when she allowed those memories to intrude easily put paid to that assumption, but she refused to dwell on
that one small flaw in her reasoning.

Not long after lunch a month before the magazine was
due to recommence publication Keira had been down to
check on some copy-editing. She stepped into the lift and
absently pressed the button for the twelfth floor. As she
skimmed through her notes the lift sped silently upwards
and when it stopped she looked up, prepared to step into
the hallway to her office, but the panel indicated she had
halted on the tenth floor.

The lift doors slid silently open and the object of Keira's
recurring tortured thoughts stood before her, framed in the
aperture.

In simply a split-second she knew her well-intentioned
rationalisation of their indiscreet interlude those short weeks
ago exploded into a million meaningless fragments.

She heard once more the sensual sound of the material

of his trousers rasping against her nylons as his leg slid between hers. She felt again the solid strength of his broad chest, his arms wrapped possessively around her.

Remembering, her breasts swelled beneath the thin cotton of her tailored shirt, her nipples throbbing sensitively as they responded, and she lifted the sheaf of papers in her hand in an effort to disguise their disconcerting perfidy.

And his mouth. She was almost lost in the recollected sensations of the seductive excitement of his lips moving on hers. Keira felt herself groan inside, part electrifying recall and part painful reminder.

That embrace had been no figment of her fanciful imagination. It was as real as he was, standing before her, over six feet of charismatic male magnetism.

Her heartbeats raced and for one wildly unrestrained moment she wanted only to fall literally into his arms, lose herself in the exhilaration of their physical attraction.

Then reality was thankfully restored and she took a grip on her impetuous impulses. That they'd meet somewhere, some time, in this building, had been unavoidable. At least now the intoxicating ''any moment now'' could fade into the prosaic ''been and gone''.

Then, to her consternation, Eden stepped into the cubicle to join her, and its spaciousness suddenly diminished with her misguided justification.

While part of Keira, the blatantly physical sensation section she seemed to have trouble quelling these days, stood on attentive alert, her conscious mind absurdly demanded to know why he wasn't using his exclusive penthouse lift.

''You have a very expressive face,'' he remarked softly, and Keira's eyes rose to meet his.

''Really?'' she stated, thrown conversationally off balance for a moment before she recovered her poise. ''No doubt you'll tell me what you thought I was thinking.''

''Why isn't he using the executive lift?'' He repeated her

silent speculation almost verbatim and, taken aback by his perception, Keira shrugged off-handedly.

"It's your building."

"Yes, it is that." He gave a soft laugh. "And the implication is that as I'm the king of this particular castle I can use any part of my kingdom I choose to."

Or anyone, Keira's fertile mind expanded, setting off a titillating trail of tantalising memories that only served to raise her ire. And that it was directed at herself didn't dim her ill-humour at all. She couldn't prevent her stormy grey eyes from raking him. And the king would so enjoy the divine droit de seigneur, she mused testily.

Eden's dark eyebrows rose. "Now that was an interesting thought." He raised his firm chin and his lips twitched into an almost-smile. "Perhaps I should take you up on that."

"On what? I have no idea what you're talking about."

"Don't you? I think you do."

"If you consider yourself so good at guessing games then perhaps you should put your talent to better use," Keira said acidly. "On the horses, maybe?" She arched a scathing brow.

"Gambling? A mug's game. Although I'll admit it has some entertainment value."

"Yes. I saw you being entertained at the last Melbourne Cup."

"You were there?" he asked, leaning casually on the chrome handrail that skirted the cubicle.

His immaculate pale grey jacket opened to display a matching waistcoat over a pale blue shirt, and his maroon tie bore a crest Keira couldn't identify. But there was one thing she did recall. Her mind flashed her a vivid picture from that afternoon in her office, of her trembling fingers fumbling to unbutton his waistcoat.

And, dear lord, she yearned to do it again. Run her fingertips over the hard muscles beneath his silk shirt, slip them inside to...

Keira swallowed and patted agitatedly at some fine tendrils of hair that had escaped her chignon and were teasing her skin. At least, she told herself it was those wayward strands.

More scenes played in her mind's eye. Eden's lips on the spot where her fingers now brushed... She moved her position hastily to disguise the shivers of pleasure her memories were evoking.

But he was looking at her, waiting for her reply. What had he said? She swallowed again and angrily chastised herself.

"At the Melbourne Cup? No, I wasn't there. I saw you on the television coverage." Some of her ire overflowed to centre on him. He was to blame, she told herself irrationally, and her anger loosened her tongue. "You were with the current Miss Australia, I believe," she added and then wished she could have bitten back the revealing postscript.

"You have a good memory," he said easily.

"And no doubt you'd forgotten."

"No. What red-blooded man could forget such an attractive young woman?"

Fingers of pain seemed to wrap around Keira's heart and she tore her gaze from his in case he read the anguish she suspected was all too visible in their smoky depths.

"Another instance of things not being quite what they seemed. It was part of a promotion for charity," he continued, and Keira, in command of herself once more, looked up. "We stood about and made fascinating small talk while the cameras rolled. Then she went off with her very attentive boyfriend and I went down to place a couple of bets. For entertainment's sake," he added, and Keira could have sworn his blue eyes twinkled.

Whatever happened, it reduced her knees to water and caused a rather different sort of pain to swell in her breast. In fact it was more pleasure than pain, she admitted, as it spread like wildfire, stirring in the pit of her stomach and reminding her again just how physically attracted to this man she was.

"I lost," he said and, totally disconcerted, Keira blinked inanely at him.

"My bets on the Cup," he explained. "So my guesses don't always strike true. But then again, I didn't get to see the horses' faces."

Keira felt her lips tighten. He was so enjoying getting his amusement at her expense, she told herself, while part of her demanded to know why her sense of humour deserted her when she was with him.

As she sought a cutting rejoinder she sensed him move and her startled gaze rose. He'd pushed himself upright and as if in slow motion his hand reached out to follow the path of her own fingers only moments before.

He touched one soft curl of her hair, lifted it, his eyes narrowed now as they centred on the curve of her neck where the errant wisp had rested. Gently he tucked it back into place and his fingers then trailed over her bare skin.

Keira's senses came alive, and just as her perfidious body began to respond she made herself jerk away from him, her papers falling from her suddenly nerveless fingers in the process.

Pages scattered about them on to the carpeted floor of the lift and they bent down as one to gather them up. Their fingers reached together, touched, and a jolt of electricity seemed to arc between them. They both stilled, their gazes locked, and Keira saw and recognised the same flame of passion in his darkened eyes. The fire of desire was burning furiously within them both.

Keira gulped a breath, knowing she had to douse the blaze before it took hold... But her whole body seemed paralysed. Her lips parted slightly and Eden's eyes were drawn to her mouth, then fell lower to settle on the pulse that beat wildly at the base of her throat.

Her cream shirt afforded him a tantalising glimpse of the

swell of her breasts and she had to put her other hand to the floor to steady herself as she felt herself falter vertiginously.

Then she noticed that the hem of her salmon-coloured straight skirt had risen high on her thighs and, fumbling with her notes, she made to pull it back into some semblance of modesty. Of course this only served to draw Eden's attention to her nylon-clad legs, and she took a shallow breath as she forced herself shakily to her feet.

Slowly he recovered the rest of her papers and with a wry twist of his lips he handed them back to her.

Neither of them had noticed that the lift had stopped or that the doors had opened with a refined ding. Only when the doors began to close again did Eden move to punch the button to prevent them.

"Your floor, I think, Keira." He motioned gallantly for her to leave and Keira barely suppressed a sigh of relief as she walked out of the lift to safety.

However, her relief was of the short-lived variety because he moved into the hallway behind her.

Keira's step faltered and she turned to face him. "Where are you going?" she asked, and then mentally winced. She had no right to question the head of the corporation, regardless of what she thought of him. He was her boss, and, as she'd stated before, this was his building.

"The same place you are, I imagine." He raised his arm and flicked back his pale blue cuff to glance at his wristwatch. "And we're five minutes late."

"Late?" Keira repeated. "Late for what?"

"For our meeting. Two p.m. in the conference room."

Keira frowned.

"It would appear you didn't receive my memo."

She shook her head. "No. There's been no memo. Not that I've seen, anyway."

"Megan sent it down to Denver's office yesterday and I

could scarcely see him forgetting to pass it on to you and the rest of the staff.''

"I'm sorry. There's been a mistake made somewhere,'' Keira said hurriedly. "If you'd care to go along to the conference room I'll tell everyone you're here. If that's all right with you,'' she added as evenly as she could, and he nodded.

"I suppose it will have to be, won't it? I'll see you in there.''

With that he left her and Keira spent a few seconds staring after him before she was galvanised into action. Racing through the office she sent everyone after Eden. However, when she stuck her head into Roxie's office her assistant wasn't at her desk.

"Damn!'' Keira said under her breath and continued into her own office next door. She'd have to leave a message for Roxie to tell her to join the meeting as soon as possible.

Keira lifted some papers on her desk but could see no memo. She found a notepad, but before she could put pen to paper Roxie herself appeared in the doorway.

"Hi, Keira! How did it go with the copy-editing?'' The other girl strolled into Keira's office.

"Oh, Roxie. Thank heavens. I thought you might have gone out. Where were you?''

"Even I need to go to the little girls' room occasionally,'' Roxie commented wryly. "I might have known something drastic would happen if I left the confines of my desk. What's up? Good grief!'' she exclaimed. "That threatened distributors' strike hasn't come to fruition, has it?''

"No. Almost worse than that. Did you see a memo about a meeting today with Eden Cassidy?'' Keira moved quickly around her desk as the other girl shook her head.

"Are you kidding? If I'd seen a memo from the big white chief himself I'd have claimed it and had it framed as a memento.''

"Heaven only knows what happened to it. It was supposed to have come down yesterday."

"Don't tell me we've missed seeing Eden Cassidy?" Roxie asked as she went to sit down.

Keira forestalled her by taking her arm and turning her around. "No time to sit, Roxie. Let's go. They're waiting for us in the conference room."

"Who are?"

"The rest of the crew. And Eden Cassidy."

"Eden Cassidy. Here? In the flesh? Why didn't you say so? My prayers are answered." Roxie gazed momentarily skywards. "So what are we lingering here for, Keira? Come on, let's start the stampede."

Suppressing a giggle that threatened to burst from her at Roxie's humour, Keira felt some of her tension abate just a little. The shadow of a smile still lit her face as she opened the door but it faded quickly as she led the way into the large room where the rest of the staff and Eden Cassidy awaited them.

She refused to allow herself to look directly at Eden for fear the shadows of those heady moments in the elevator would be clearly visible on her face for all to see. Yet still she couldn't prevent the telltale colour washing her warm cheeks.

"Ah, Keira." Denver stood up from his position at Eden's right hand. "Some wires seem to have managed to get crossed somewhere along the track."

"Yes," Keira replied without intonation as she slid quickly into her seat, "apparently they have."

"No matter. We're all here now." Eden waved recriminations aside. "Let's get down to business. Are we on track for publication date?"

For the next two hours Eden questioned them relentlessly about every facet of the progress of the magazine and, although they could have continued, promptly at five o'clock Eden drew the meeting to a close. There were thankful sighs

as chairs scraped and paper rustled as they all began to file
out of the conference room.

"Keira. One minute." Eden's deep voice stopped Keira
as she made to follow the rest of the staff.

As Keira's step faltered, Denver and Roxie turned back,
their facial expressions registering surprise. Roxie recovered
enough to give Keira an audacious wink before she continued on her way, while Denver's thin lips tightened in a far
less indulgent manner. Keira's flush was the resulting sum
total of both of their so obvious sentiments.

"Yes, Mr Cassidy?" Keira projected her voice to reach
the ears of the retreating Denver Clarkson. At least she knew
she could explain the real situation to Roxie later.

Eden folded his arms casually as he leant back against
the conference table.

He didn't immediately break the silence, making her feel
uneasily aware of their isolation, and that same revealing
pulse began to beat at the base of her throat.

"Were you wanting some more information?" Keira
asked quickly, and he grimaced.

"Yes. In a manner of speaking, I was." His dark gaze
held hers. "Have dinner with me, hmm?"

CHAPTER EIGHT

"DINNER?" Keira repeated, completely taken aback. Whatever she had expected him to ask her, it certainly wasn't that.

"Dinner. Tonight." His deep voice played over her, rousing her senses and lowering her defences.

Its huskiness stirred her fertile imagination and she could almost smell the faint scent of roses, see a secluded table for two, an unobtrusive waiter pouring wine. And catch the dark, glimmering sparkle of Eden's eyes in the flickering candlelight.

Why not? persuaded one part of her, the part that housed her traitorous longings. Why not grasp the chance and run with it? Experience all that he offered for as long as it lasted? At least then she'd have the memories to savour when it was over.

When it was over, reiterated her level-headed conscious mind.

A brief affair. Romantic. Exciting. And physically satisfying. She was so very sure it would be that.

So why not? Her incited nerve-endings increased threefold the intoxicating temptation to accept his invitation. Yes, it would be a mutually satisfying affair. But an affair for all that. With her boss.

"Well, Keira?" he prompted, and Keira drew her wildly conflicting thoughts into some semblance of order, her grey eyes meeting his.

"I'm sorry. I can't."

"Can't or won't?"

Keira shrugged. "Both."

"Because of the gossip?"

"No. Yes." She fidgeted with her papers, betraying her agitation.

"No one need know," he said easily, and Keira gave a soft, sceptical laugh.

"Someone would find out, believe me. They always do."

"And you're going to allow what other people think to govern your life, what you do and don't do?" he asked with an ominous quietness.

"That makes me sound spineless, and I'm not." Keira lifted her chin boldly.

It was his turn to give an incredulous laugh. "Spineless would not be a term that would come to my mind to describe you, Keira. But perhaps you *are* a little too anxious about what other people think."

"I'm afraid I can't help that. I do care about how others see me. And I dislike immensely the idea that the general consensus might be that I schemed to get this job."

Eden made a negating movement with his hand. "We've been through this before. And I can assure you that anyone who knows me would realise I don't make a habit of allowing my—" he paused "—personal life to influence a decision that might reflect badly on my business. I'm no philanthropist, nor am I a philanderer. You wouldn't have this position if I didn't think you were more than qualified to do it. So shall we acknowledge that point as being on the record?"

"Maybe I don't want to join the queue…"

A frown of irritation settled on Eden's brow.

"Or perhaps I just don't want to go with you," Keira continued quickly, her gaze holding his momentarily before her eyes fell.

"Don't you?" he asked, the softly spoken words reaching into her soul, twisting, negating her small spurt of bravado.

His eyebrows rose mockingly at her hesitation and she felt her anger flare. "All right. If things were different, well, I'd consider accepting. But as it is I'm not going to," she finished with conviction.

"What are you really afraid of, Keira?" he asked imperiously. "Public opinion? Or yourself?"

Her grey eyes rose to meet his again. "What are you talking about?"

"I'm talking about the way we strike sparks off each other. The way the air between us almost ignites with the electrical charge we generate." He gave a quick derisive smile. "For some reason it seems to alarm you. I repeat, what are you afraid of?"

"If you mean am I afraid of you, then all I can say is you're flattering yourself."

"Look, Keira," he continued, letting her jibe go over his head, "I don't know what sort of relationships you've had in the past but—"

"My past relationships have nothing whatsoever to do with you," Keira declared indignantly.

"Don't they? Then that sets a precedent. Now you don't get to throw mine and the critical way you mistakenly see them into the conversation either. So we forget about queues."

His composed, supercilious smile fanned her anger. "I think you're suffering from the too-rich syndrome," she threw at him furiously. "Too much, too many, too often. Unfortunately, what it all boils down to is that the decision is mine to make. Negative or positive. And I choose not to. If your ego can't accept that decision then that's tough and I'm sorry."

He unfolded his arms, straightening from where he'd been casually leaning against the conference table, and Keira had the unnerving feeling he was uncoiling like a lithe snake about to strike. Her nerves gave an apprehensive tremble but she made herself hold her ground.

"However, don't despair," she continued tersely, the corners of her mouth lifting in a tense, humourless smile. "As the saying goes, there are plenty more fish in the sea."

He gave a faint shake of his head and began to walk past her. But when he paused beside her, his hard body mere millimetres from hers, her breath caught agitatedly in her throat.

Firm fingers took hold of her chin and before she could draw back he had pressed a quick hard kiss on her parted lips.

"I hate fishing," he said evenly as he left her.

And how she wished she could give the next few hours a very wide berth, Keira thought a couple of weeks later as she dressed for the flashy cocktail party that had been organised to launch *Natural Life*.

A reception-room in one of the city's most prestigious hotels had been hired for the evening and the entire staff had been looking forward to the occasion for weeks. Not so Keira.

By all accounts everybody would be there. Including Eden Cassidy.

She hadn't seen her boss since the afternoon in the conference-room when he'd asked her to have dinner with him, although an invitation to a dinner party at his apartment last week had been extended to her. Daniel had informed her twenty or so people from the publishing industry were attending, and she told herself her main reason for declining was to quell any lingering gossip about her relationship with Eden.

Reaching behind her, Keira zipped up her dress, glancing in the mirror critically as she adjusted the thin straps. The wine-red sheath flattered her figure, she knew, and the rich, deep colour accentuated the pale skin of her shoulders. She slipped on the all-but-transparent matching short-sleeved jacket that went with the outfit, and sighed.

Although she knew she felt comfortable about her appearance, she wished for the hundredth time she didn't have to go. This sort of thing, the public relations exercise to help sell their magazine, wasn't her scene at all. She was far happier in her office doing what she knew she did well.

Keira clasped on her earrings, small diamond pendants that drew attention to the curve of her neck, and she turned her head slightly to check that her loose chignon was still in place. A few softening wisps curled down from her temples and she patted them absently.

She had applied only the minimum of make-up, a little eyeshadow to her lids and mascara to her fair lashes, and her lipstick complemented the colour of her dress. Just her shoes and she was ready.

She glanced at her dress watch and flicked off the bedroom light. Roxie would be collecting her any moment. As she walked down the hallway the cat wound himself with intricate precision between her feet.

"I just want you to know, Roger," she said, bending down to tickle him under his chin, "that the only reason I'm going tonight is to keep you in gourmet cat food."

The cat made a mrrrr! of disbelief, flicked his tail and then stalked back towards his food bowl, obviously deciding to take advantage of its offering while it was available. Keira was still smiling when Roxie tooted her car horn outside.

An accident on the arterial road delayed Keira and Roxie, so the party was in full swing by the time the two women arrived at the prestigious hotel.

As a waiter passed, Roxie grabbed two glasses of wine from his tray, handing one to Keira.

"Cheers. Here's to an evening of perfect and widespread publicity," she said as she raised her glass, and Keira made a face.

"And may the evening pass swiftly," she muttered with feeling.

"Just relax and enjoy," Roxie admonished, and then turned slightly. "Oh ho. Here comes Dingbat Di. Sorry to desert you, Keira, but I feel a sudden urge to mingle elsewhere. See you, and good luck." With that Roxie vanished into the crowd.

"Hello, Keira." Dianna Forester's eyes skimmed Keira's dark red dress but her expression gave nothing away. "An impressive turn-out."

"Yes." Keira sipped her wine. "The public relations people have done a great job."

"So it would seem. Anybody who's anybody is here." Dianna paused. "Including Eden Cassidy himself."

At the mention of his name Keira felt warm colour flood her face and she cringed inwardly in dismay as the other girl's dark eyes narrowed. "I think Daniel did say that his uncle might come along," she put in quickly, suspecting she was betraying herself with every passing second.

"Eden Cassidy in himself is always newsworthy and the place is alive with any reporter who's anybody," Dianna remarked. "It certainly won't hurt to have his clout behind the magazine launch."

"No. I suppose it won't." Keira swallowed another mouthful of her wine, her dry mouth not tasting the liquid.

"It was Eden's idea to recommence publication of *Natural Life*, wasn't it?" Dianna asked and Keira nodded.

"I think it was."

"Strange that a man in his position should become involved in what can only be described as a very small pebble in his media conglomerate."

"I wouldn't say so, Dianna. Eden Cassidy gives me the impression that he's very well informed about every last section of his business. I'd imagine a man in his position would have to be."

"Perhaps." Dianna pursed her lips. "Yet in all the years I've worked on *Chloe* I only ever saw him at general meetings. And even then he rarely singled out any one particular publication.''

Keira shrugged, searching the crowd valiantly for an excuse to escape a conversation that was getting far too uncomfortable for her.

"Something must have piqued his interest," Dianna continued. "Or someone," she added with apparently deliberate balefulness.

Keira's eyes snapped to meet the other woman's and she drew herself up to her full height. "What exactly do you mean, Dianna?" she asked just as quietly.

"Why, nothing. We all think it's wonderful that the big chief is taking such a personal interest in *Natural Life*."

"I'd hardly call it a personal interest," Keira began and Dianna laughed softly.

"Don't be so defensive, Keira. Just take advantage of it while you can. Opportunity only knocks once in a long while and you'd be a fool not to grab it when it's available."

"Look, Dianna. If you or anyone else think there was anything unprofessional about my appointment as editor of *Natural Life*, then let me assure you you couldn't be more wrong."

Dianna's eyes moved slightly, her focus shifting, and her thin lips moved upwards in a welcoming smile. "Eden. Nice to see you. Another successful launch, it would seem," she effervesced easily.

Keira's entire body stiffened as she sensed Eden Cassidy's presence behind her. Her whole nervous system jumped to attention and her fingers tightened on her wine glass until she feared it would snap under the strain.

Then to her horror his hand clasped her arm, his fingers encircling her bare flesh, burning where they touched her. Tingles of fire raced up her arm, engulfed her, and it took her all her power to prevent herself from flinching away from him. He manoeuvred himself through the throng of people around them and only when he stood facing them both did he release Keira from his searing hold.

"Keira." His deep vibrant voice tantalised her already aroused nerve-endings as he acknowledged her with a faint inclination of his dark head.

"Good evening, Mr Cassidy," she managed to get out, and Dianna's gaze shifted with swift speculation from one to the other.

Eden's sensuous lips twitched wryly and his slightly narrowed eyes conveyed that he recognised the formality of her greeting. "Can I get you both another glass of wine?" he asked, but before either Keira or Dianna could reply Daniel broke out of the crowd and slapped his uncle good-naturedly on the back.

"What a crush," he said and then turned to the other woman. "Glad I found you, Dianna. Denver Clarkson's been looking for you. Something about some prospective advertisers for *Chloe*, I think."

Dianna excused herself with obvious reluctance and left them.

"Hi, Keira!" Daniel ran his eyes over Keira's outfit and whistled softly. "Wow! You look great."

"For an old broad?" Keira finished, and he laughed.

"Yeah. Exactly. Well, I guess the magazine's going to be a winner if tonight's anything to go by." Daniel beamed at his uncle, apparently undaunted by Eden's obvious disapproval of the easy banter between Keira and his nephew. "So it would seem this might be the best time to ask for a raise in pay." He winked at Keira before turning back to Eden. "What do you say?"

"I'd say not a particularly good taste comment when you take into consideration the industrial action that's pending," his uncle remarked drily.

"Oops! Bad timing on my part. Sorry, Eden. I forgot about the distributors being restless. I'd better change the subject. Something funny just happened," he chattered on.

"Someone asked me to introduce them to Aunt Aggie but I didn't want to spoil their image of her. You know, grey hair, glasses on the end of her nose, short and grandmotherly."

"And she isn't?" Eden remarked, and Daniel chuckled.

"Shall I tell him, Keira?"

Keira shrugged and Daniel made a flourishing movement with his hand toward her.

"Eden Cassidy, meet Aunt Aggie Rains."

Eden raised his dark brows. "You write that column?"

Keira nodded.

"Yet another of your many talents?"

"Sure is," Daniel put in delightedly.

"I use my aunt's diaries and recipe books." Keira explained, just a little flushed with embarrassment. "She was very particular about recording everything."

"Keira doesn't exactly fit the picture, does she?" Daniel laughed again and continued as Keira's colour deepened. "Blushing becomes you," he said with flamboyant aplomb.

"Enough, Daniel," Eden warned.

"Sorry, Keira," Daniel apologised. "Time for another subject change." He turned back to his uncle. "So, what's this I hear about Megan being in New York?"

"She left yesterday," Eden told him dispassionately, his eyes still moving over Keira's face, and she shifted uneasily, hoping Daniel would be too involved in his own concerns to notice his uncle's so obvious attention.

"I expected Megan to be here with bells on," Daniel was probing. "What's she doing in New York?"

"She wanted to see a Broadway show," his uncle replied tartly.

"Very droll, Eden. When's she due back?"

"Although I can't understand your sudden interest in Megan, and apart from its not being any of your business, Daniel, she'll be tied up for a few weeks."

"A few weeks," Daniel repeated in amazement as he

raised his eyebrows at his uncle. "You mean we're launching this magazine without Megan's good right hand? Well, the indispensable becomes dispensable."

"Now there's an idea," said Eden meaningfully. "It may not be such a good idea to put such interesting thoughts into my mind."

Daniel raised his hands in mock horror. "Then by all means consider it not said. Think I'll quit while I'm ahead. See you two later," he added as he left them.

Keira's mouth went suddenly dry and she made herself move, lifted her wine glass to her lips, and then felt herself colour as she realised the glass was empty.

Eden reached out and took the glass from her nerveless fingers as a waiter materialised beside them. And Keira was too stunned to refuse the refill.

"Denver tells me everything's gone to plan with the magazine," he remarked casually and Keira nodded, feeling more than one pair of eyes watching them with interest.

"Yes. There have been no real problems," she said uneasily, and then pulled herself together. "Well, I guess I should leave you to mingle," she added brightly and made to move away.

"You didn't come to the party I gave last week," he said conversationally and Keira stopped, her muscles tensing.

"No. Thank you for asking me but I'd made other plans," she replied without intonation. She'd sent her inability to accept via Daniel, and this time Keira had refused to allow the young man to talk her into changing her mind and going.

"So Daniel informed me." He paused. "He said you had a date."

Keira met his narrowed gaze, remembering her excuse. She'd told Daniel she intended to curl up with a good book. Scarcely a date. And Daniel knew that. So what was Daniel playing at?

"Who was he?" The even timbre of Eden's voice repudiated the stormy darkness of his eyes and Keira's throat contracted.

For long moments she was unable to formulate a reply. "Daniel had no right to tell you anything." She drew a quick, steadying breath. "And apart from that I hardly think it's any of your business how I spend my weekends."

Eden Cassidy might be her boss but he didn't own her free time. He'd issued invitations and she'd refused. If he couldn't take no for an answer that was his problem. She had no intention of allowing him to intimidate her in any way. And telling herself that was fine, she acknowledged, but now she had to put her resolve into practice.

Eden's eyes were impaling hers and she found she was powerless to break their hold over her.

"He doesn't seem to be dancing attendance tonight," he said at last, in that same portentous tone.

"Who?" Keira got out through tense lips.

"Your date," he repeated laconically.

The temperature in the room had become stifling and Keira yearned to race for the doorway, draw some cooling air into her tortured lungs. She swallowed and took hold of what little of her composure remained intact.

"Perhaps he isn't insecure enough in himself to feel the need to bind me to his side," she said scathingly. And she had the exhilarating sensation of knowing her barb had found its target as he lifted his head, his strong jaw clenching.

"Do I take that as a critique of my character? Or apparent lack of it," he added caustically, and Keira shrugged.

"Take it any way you feel you need to take it," she expounded with a coolly insolent smile.

"Oh, believe me, Keira, I wouldn't need to bind you to my side," he said proprietorially. "You simply wouldn't want to leave."

"What an illuminating statement," Keira threw back at

him. "And even more so because I think you really believe
that."

He gave a quietly humourless laugh. "And you believe
it too, Keira."

His vibrant voice, soft as velvet now, made her body tingle right down to her toes, and she clutched at her anger to
conceal the betrayal of her seditious senses.

"I can't believe your arrogance, your—"

"We could put it to the test," he cut in. "Care to try to
prove me wrong, Keira?"

"No," she replied with as much dignity as she could
muster. "Unfortunately, I can't help your mistaken assump-
tions. And quite frankly, I don't really care what you think.
Now, I've been neglecting the other guests—"

"And especially your escort."

Keira raised her chin. "The other guests," she repeated
composedly, her grey gaze boldly holding his.

"Who is he?" he reiterated with almost tangible con-
straint, and they stood facing each other like incited adver-
saries about to do battle.

"Is the relationship serious?" he asked at last, when
Keira was sure the gathering tension between them was
about to explode into a million pieces.

She opened her mouth to tell him it was, to provide herself with some cover to hide behind, to cloak her very real
and frightening attraction to this man. But somehow the
words wouldn't come. And he read the truth in her eyes
before she could disguise it.

He smiled then, a magnanimously satisfied expression of
triumph, and Keira had to fight the urge to lash out physically at him.

"You are the most egotistical, insufferable, objectionable
man it has ever been my misfortune to meet," she got out
through clenched teeth, and went to swing away from him.

But his strong hand reached out, fingers clasping her arm
to stay her, and Keira raised her furious gaze to his.

"Please don't do that," she whispered tersely, barely controlling her temper, but also aware just how close she and Eden were to making a scene.

"Do what?"

"That," Keira repeated, and tried to ease her arm from his touch, but his fingers tightened. "You're embarrassing me."

"By talking to you?" he said infuriatingly. "Surely as your boss I'd be expected to have things to discuss with you."

"Talking to me? Your topics of conversation leave a lot to be desired. Now, I suggest you let me go." Her eyes went expressively to the place where his fingers held her arm. And she made herself ignore the fact that her so-reponsive nerve-endings where he touched her bare skin had set up a wild tattoo which was spreading like a fireball. "Let me go, Eden," she repeated. "Everyone will begin to wonder about—well…" Keira paused, colour washing her face again.

"Ah!" he exclaimed, his tone infuriatingly placating. "Everyone will begin to wonder. And if someone sees me touching your arm they'll expect me to give you a television station of your own."

With prolonged deliberation he slowly released her, only to trail one strong finger down the length of her arm to her wrist, settling momentarily on the soft flesh where her pulse raced, before eventually breaking the contact. "Heaven only knows what might happen if that someone saw me put my arm around you," he added drily and Keira's eyes flashed angrily.

"Someone? Good grief! There are hundreds of people here and you can't really imagine you aren't the focus of most of their attention."

"If I went around thinking that I'd be accused of being an egomaniac."

Keira raised her chin eloquently and he gave a softly sensual laugh. "Such flattery, my dear Keira. Must I add that to your list of my failings?"

"Perhaps your biggest failing is that you've spent so much time in your ivory tower you've forgotten, if you ever knew, about the intrigues of the lower rank and file. You're perfectly safe in your penthouse, Mr Cassidy, but I have to live and work down here."

"The casting couch again?" he said with that same dangerous quietness, all humour washed from his expression.

Keira's gaze met his in trepidation but she stood her ground. "You know exactly what I mean."

"I still think you're over-reacting."

"And I've already had to defend myself once tonight. I don't need any more drama to fuel the flame."

His dark head rose as he frowned. "Be specific, Keira. Who and what?"

"I don't choose to tell you."

"If you're talking about Denver Clarkson, then let me just say he has a very sick wife so I'm sure he's got more to worry about than my sex-life. Or lack of it," he added incitingly, and Keira felt her mouth tighten in exasperation.

"I think I can safely say this particular person was simply speaking for the majority and and leave it at that," Keira said bitterly, and he shoved his hands in his pockets.

"Then perhaps I should make a public announcement and settle this once and for all. Keira Strong got this job because she was the best person to fill it. No sexual favours have been exchanged."

Keira flushed and glanced quickly around to see if anyone had heard his outrageous words. "Do you have to be so offensive? We're attracting more than enough attention as it is."

His blue eyes glittered dangerously. "We could attract a hell of a lot more," he said and stepped closer, his eyes burning into hers, his suit-clad chest just millimetres from her suddenly taut and throbbing breasts.

"Eden, please..."

"Please?" he repeated shortly. "Please." His deep tone fell intoxicatingly. "That's what I'd like to do. Please you. And I promise you, I would."

Keira's heartbeats drummed at his sensual tone, his arousing words, and she shook her head desperately. "Eden, don't. I can't take this any more."

"You can't take it? Don't you know you're driving me crazy? Come with me after the launch. We'll have some supper."

Her heartbeats caught painfully in her throat and she felt decidedly light-headed. "You know I can't do that," she got out through her dry lips.

"Do I? I don't, you know. And neither do you. Forget everyone else. Think about yourself. Do it for yourself. You know you want to." His low, erotic intonation played over her and she felt her quivering, insidious senses clamour for her surrender. And she knew she was rapidly forgetting the reasons why she was denying herself the electrifying pleasure of submission. Why not let him take her anywhere he chose, satisfy the spreading fire within her?

Desperately she shook her head and the wisps of fair hair escaping from her chignon teased her neck, again reminding her of the touch of his lips.

"Come with me," he repeated urgently, the words flowing over her like warm oil, tantalising, enticing her.

CHAPTER NINE

"No!" THE word broke softly from her. "I...I can't," she said again with a little more composure.

"For God's sake, Keira," he ground out, running his hand impassionedly through his hair. His gaze held hers, and for immeasurable seconds pierced her with his controlled fury. "I think I need some air," he said at last, and strode away from her without a backward glance or the slightest concern about how his abrupt departure would appear to those nearby.

"What was that all about?" Roxie asked as she joined Keira, her eyes on Eden's retreating figure.

Keira took a careful sip of her wine before replying. "I guess he has other people to see. He's a very busy man."

"And not a happy one, it would seem." Roxie turned back to Keira. "So the question is, did he leave or was he asked to go?"

"I haven't the faintest idea what you're talking about, Roxie."

"Ah, she knows nothing. Look, Keira, one piece of advice. Don't go missing the flowers for the trees."

Keira raised her eyebrows and Roxie shrugged.

"Or something like that. Eden Cassidy's not a man to be manipulated. Plain as Aunt Aggie's down-to-earth advice."

"I'm not trying to manipulate anyone, Rox. And you know I don't mix business with pleasure."

"I'd be surprised if you remembered what that sort of pleasure was," remarked the other girl outrageously.

"Roxie! Enough."

"OK. OK. But I, and the rest of the female population of Australia for that matter, can't see what you've got against the man."

"Against him? Well, for a start, he's a playboy. Only masochists get involved with known playboys. I'm not a masochist. And I don't want to become one of his harem."

"Harem? Aren't you being a little over the top? I mean, he just doesn't seem that type to me. I know I rave about him being good-looking. He's surely that. But quite seriously, Keira, he couldn't run a corporation this big so successfully if he persisted in love-'em-and-leave-'em dalliances. He has to put in the time, if you get what I mean."

"There's such a thing as delegation, Roxie. And anyway, you're forgetting Megan Donnelly."

"He'd be a fool to tamper with her. And he's not a fool," Roxie dismissed. "Good secretaries, and from what I hear she's the best, aren't that thick on the ground. Apart from that, I've heard she's almost a couple with a friend of Eden's in the States."

"Well, don't try to tell me you haven't seen the bevy of beauties who flock around him." Keira saw her argument slipping out from under her. "They're here in force tonight. And there's nary a week goes past that the newspapers and glossies don't feature a shot of him with a different model on his arm."

"You even made it one week," Roxie reminded her drily, and Keira glanced at her sharply. "So, did that picture tell a story?" Roxie asked as Keira set her wine glass down on a nearby table.

"You know I just happened to be standing near him when—"

"I rest my case." Roxie cut in quickly. "How many other times have the beauties just happened to have been standing near him when?" Roxie mimicked Keira's words.

"He's my boss, Roxie."

"So what?"

"You know so what. I'd hazard a guess that there are more people here tonight who think I got this job by foul means rather than fair. In fact Dianna all but spelled it out."

"Then she got it wrong. Anyway, everyone knows her nose is out of joint because she's lost the best slave she's ever had, namely you, Keira Strong. Besides, those of us who work with you haven't got a problem about why you're the editor. We know you deserved it."

"Oh, come on, Roxie. Surely you've heard the rumours—"

"Rumours be damned! That's your smokescreen. What's the real reason you're at such pains to pretend indifference to the man? And don't tell me you find him unattractive or we'll have you certified."

"Perhaps I haven't got time for that sort of distraction," Keira began, wondering what Roxie would say if she knew she was only repeating Eden's own suspicions.

Roxie gave a snicker. "Nonsense."

"I've worked hard to get where I am and I don't want to jeopardise it by having a meaningless affair with the one person who can terminate my employment on the spot."

"It's Dennis, isn't it?"

"Dennis?" Keira raised her eyebrows in surprise at Roxie's change of tack.

"I know you had a rough time with him. Your ex-husband was a selfish little wimp who wanted a mother, not a wife. But you can't let that spoil your chances for a totally different relationship."

Keira sighed. "I don't deny that for a while my marriage to Dennis did colour my feelings about getting involved again. However, I've come to terms with all that. I'm older now and hopefully wiser."

"So you must know there's no comparison between Eden Cassidy and Dennis," Roxie continued determinedly. "Dennis was spineless but there isn't a weak bone in Eden's body. Have you ever read anything unsavoury about the man?''

Keira shook her head tiredly.

"That's because he has integrity.''

"Roxie,'' Keira appealed, feeling the beginnings of a headache. If only she could slip away. But of course she couldn't. Not now that Eden had left. It would look far too suspicious.

"All right. I'm sorry, Keira. I've probably said more than enough already. But I care about you and I don't want to see you throw away your chance of happiness because you're afraid to meet life head on.''

"At the risk of provoking you into further wise counsel, Roxie, I'd just like to say I'd prefer simply to jog quietly along beside life for a while. Now, let's get a cup of coffee before all this stress and the two glasses of wine I've had go to my head.''

Roxie had just left Keira to fetch the coffee when Meg, one of Keira's receptionists, approached with an attractive young woman who looked more than a little ill at ease.

"Have you seen Daniel?'' Meg asked and Keira shook her head.

"Not for a while. But he shouldn't be far away.'' She looked around but couldn't see Eden's nephew in the throng of people.

"I'll see if I can find him for you,'' Meg offered as she turned to the young girl. "If you'd like to stay with Keira, I won't be long.''

Keira glanced back at the other girl questioningly.

"I'm Cat. Cat Craigie,'' she said softly, her fingers playing nervously with the thin strap of her bag.

Keira took in Daniel's young friend and realised she was indeed looking at a younger version of herself. Cat was almost as tall as Keira but she wore her fair hair, the same shade as Keira's, in natural waves to her shoulders.

"So you're Cat! I'm Keira Strong, the editor of the magazine where Daniel works.'' Keira smiled. ''It's nice to meet you at last. Daniel's told me so much about you.''

''Oh.'' Cat looked at the floor and flushed a little. ''I can't imagine what he'd say.''

''All good, I'm afraid,'' Keira laughed. ''He admires you very much.''

''Does he? I guess I'm pretty keen on Daniel too,'' she added softly before she looked up, catching Keira's eye. ''He talks a lot about you, too.''

''All good as well, I hope.''

''Yes. He likes you.

''And I like him. So that makes both of us. Daniel's pretty special.''

''I suppose,'' Cat agreed hesitantly. ''But it's all so complicated.''

''And made worse by the fact that Daniel doesn't fit the preconceived mould.''

''Yes. It would be so much easier if he was the stereotypical poor little rich kid.''

Keira smiled.

''I mean, I could handle it better if he had a silver spoon stuck in his mouth. Our lifestyles are so different it scares me. Our families, well...'' She shrugged.

''Daniel's uncle and grandfather care about him and the same goes for your parents and you. There's no difference when you get down to what counts.''

''I guess so. But we don't want any hassles that might arise because Daniel's uncle and my father are usually on opposite sides of the negotiating table.''

''I'd have said they respect each other and they usually settle any disputes reasonably amicably,'' Keira suggested gently.

Cat nodded and pulled a wry face.

''Life is fraught, isn't it?'' Keira laughed softly and Cat smiled, if somewhat reluctantly.

''I guess Daniel's worth it. Just don't tell him I said that.

nd maybe we both enjoy the intrigue.'' She grimaced.
'Well, some of the time.''

Just then Keira caught sight of Daniel weaving his way
arough the guests and she saw the beam of surprised plea-
ure that lit his face when he saw Cat. For a moment she
aought he was going to race over and embrace the young
irl but he pulled himself together and made his way non-
halantly towards them through the crowd.

''Hi, Cat. I'm glad you decided to come along.''

''Yes. I... It was kind of you to ask me. I've never been
b anything like this.'' Cat's fingers were worrying the strap
f her bag again.

''I thought you said you wouldn't be able to make it. But
'm glad you did,'' Daniel added quickly. ''Now you're
ere, would you like to meet my uncle?''

Cat drew back a little then gave Keira a quick glance
efore shaking her head. ''Well, no, Daniel. Not...''

''You have to meet him some time, so why not now?
He's not so bad, Cat. Really,'' Daniel told her and turned
b Keira for confirmation. ''Is he, Keira?''

To her consternation Keira felt herself flush and for the
ife of her she couldn't formulate an answer. What could
he say anyway? That she found Eden Cassidy almost ir-
esistibly attractive? That the moment their eyes met all her
esolute good intentions flew out of the window? And that
he suspected her capitulation to his devastating magnetism
ould become all but inevitable? *He's not so bad*. What a
readful understatement.

''In fact, I've got this great idea,'' Daniel was continuing,
naware of her inner turmoil. ''Keira can introduce you to
den.''

''Why me?'' she got out in dismay.

''Because you can wrap him around your little finger.''

''That's rubbish, Daniel. I scarcely know the man,'' Keira
rotested, her embarrassment sharpening her tone, and Cat
hifted uncomfortably from one foot to the other.

Unabashed, Daniel grinned devilishly but whatever out-rageous quip he was about to deliver was diverted when Cat touched his arm.

"Daniel, I'd just as soon not meet your uncle right now. Not yet, anyway," the younger girl said firmly. "I only came tonight because—" she paused "—I mean, I need to talk to you privately." She glanced apologetically at Keira. "If you don't mind, Keira."

"Of course not." Keira moved away, more than a little relieved to leave Daniel and his embarrassing innuendos be-hind. She wended her way in search of Roxie and the coffee but she had only had a chance to give Roxie a wave when Daniel and Cat were beside her again.

"Keira, do you know where Eden went exactly?" Daniel asked concernedly, and she shook her head.

"No. He... I think he left."

"Damn! Keira, we have to find him. And fast. Cat says..." Daniel stopped and turned back to the young girl. "I'll have to tell Keira, Cat. She should know too. OK?"

After a moment Cat nodded unhappily and Daniel sighed.

"Cat overheard her father talking to one of the union reps." Daniel had dropped his voice conspiratorially to little more than a whisper so that Keira had to strain to catch his words. "They're going out on strike. The distributors. Damn good timing, too. Just when *Natural Life* is about to hit the stands. Eden will be livid."

"I didn't want to tell Daniel," Cat said miserably. "But, well, I didn't know what to do. Oh, I just wish I hadn't overheard that conversation. But they were giving Dad a hard time and..." She shook her head and Daniel took her hand and gave it a squeeze.

"It's OK, Cat," he said consolingly and she brushed a tear from her eyes.

"I just thought that maybe Daniel's uncle and my father between them could, you know, talk some sense into them.

I only hope I've done the right thing," she finished miserably.

"Of course you have. And I know Eden'll handle it diplomatically." He looked at Keira and frowned. "Eden didn't say where he was going?"

As Keira shook her head, someone in a nearby group touched him on the shoulder.

"If you're still looking for the big chief he's in the next room. I just left him."

"Great!" Daniel exclaimed and began pushing through the crowd, pulling Cat after him.

And Keira made herself follow, albeit a little more slowly. By the time she'd reluctantly joined them Daniel had given his uncle the gist of Cat's revelations.

Eden's eyes acknowledged Keira's presence with one all-consuming glance and her knees went decidedly weak at the fire that still burned in their blue depths. Her defences sank to a new low and she experienced an urge to lean against his hard body, rest her weary head on his shoulder and take in some of his strength. So much for her determination to remain aloof from him.

Daniel was now explaining to Eden who Cat was, and his uncle regarded them both levelly.

"You don't resemble your father in the slightest," he said to Cat with a faint smile, and the young girl visibly relaxed. Then he turned back to his nephew. "We'll have a few things to discuss, Daniel, when all this is settled, hmm?"

Daniel nodded. "But what are we going to do about the strike? I mean, the magazine is supposed to hit the stands on Monday."

"I'll go and see Cat's father and between us we'll sort it out. It's probably another false alarm. A few of them tend to over-react. But if they have genuine grievances I'll listen and do my best to put them right." He ran his hand tiredly along his jaw line and then seemed to straighten before his gaze returned to Keira.

"I'll be in touch after I find out just how serious the situation is."

Keira nodded and his eyes held hers for a fraction of a second before he turned and made his way through the crowd. A few minutes later he left with Denver Clarkson and he hadn't returned before the party eventually broke up, the guests unaware of the behind-the-scenes drama.

When Roxie finally dropped Keira home she sighed with relief. Her fluctuating emotions had physically drained her. One moment she knew the excitement, the exhilaration of imagining herself surrendering to something she suspected was predestined, drowning in the promise of Eden Cassidy's so compelling charisma. The next moment she would be valiantly standing her ground, set stubbornly on not allowing herself to deviate from her decision not to succumb to his so tempting overtures.

The night had been never-ending, far more so than she could have imagined it was going to be, and then topped off by the threatened strike. All she wanted was to crawl into the sanctuary of her bed and know the oblivion of sleep. She felt as though she'd been awake for weeks and that her body had been on unalleviated alert for just as long. As long as she'd known Eden Cassidy.

After all the work that had gone into the first issue, and was going into the second issue of *Natural Life*, she knew she should be concerned about the strike delaying the magazine's release, but she felt completely numb. It was as though her awareness of Eden Cassidy and her confusion over her feelings precluded any other emotional perception.

As the tail-lights of Roxie's car disappeared down the road she swung open the gate in her high wooden fence and Roger wound himself around her legs in greeting. She closed the gate and picked him up.

"If you're wondering what sort of evening I had, then it couldn't have been worse. I'm simply exhausted and can't wait to get to bed."

And although she expected she'd lie tossing and turning, mulling over the turmoil within her, she was asleep as soon as her head touched the pillow. It seemed only moments later that she was woken by the birds greeting the morning sun and she reluctantly climbed out of bed and pulled on her short-sleeved robe. With a yawn she set the coffee-pot bubbling and went out to collect her morning newspaper.

Keira opened the gate just as Daniel's red sports car pulled into the kerb.

"Morning," he greeted her tiredly. "I've been staying at Cat's and her father just arrived home. I thought you'd like to know the strike is off."

"Oh. That's good news. Thanks, Daniel. Do you want some coffee?"

Daniel shook his head. "No. I'm bushed. I'm off home to catch up on some sleep. See you."

Keira waved as he drove off, and picked up her newspaper, only to step back in alarm when the bonnet of a dark blue Jaguar nosed into the driveway, wide tyres crunching on the gravel, passing her to draw to a stop in front of her carport.

Her hand still resting on the gate, Keira stared open-mouthed as Eden Cassidy's tall body climbed from behind the wheel and turned to face her.

He closed the car door behind him with a restrained click and leaned back against the shiny duco. "Did you manage to get any sleep last night?" he asked without inflection, his eyes running over the curve of her body beneath her towelling robe.

Keira's hand dropped from the gate to clutch together the opened V of her gown. She wore her short nightshirt beneath her robe and even though it was really quite circumspect as night attire went she felt almost naked beneath his hooded gaze.

"A little," she replied at last, taking a couple of steps toward him before stopping in confusion.

Something warned her to keep a measured distance between herself and that tall masculine body.

Yet of their own accord her eyes wandered lingeringly over him, took in his slightly dishevelled appearance. He'd shed his suit jacket and his tie, and his immaculate white shirt was open at the collar.

Her gaze met his and she swallowed, her heartbeats accelerating wildly. He'd seen her open scrutiny and she flushed disconcertedly, but he refrained from making his usual provocative comment. Instead he raised his hand to massage the back of his neck, as though to ease the tension there.

"Any chance of a cup of coffee?" he asked tiredly, and Keira almost laughed at the prosaicness of the question. Yet she paused just slightly before nodding.

Reluctantly she led the way into the house, her pulse jumping about as his footsteps followed her. Up on to the veranda. Along the seemingly mile-long hallway. Into the kitchen.

Roger stirred on the sofa and gave Eden a measuring stare, but whatever he saw must have reassured him because he tucked his nose back between his paws and resumed his snooze.

"I've just put on some coffee," she said a little breathily as she walked behind the breakfast bar. "Would you like something to eat?"

He shook his head. "No, thanks. Coffee will be fine." A strand of dark hair had fallen forward on his brow and he irritatedly brushed it back. "I thought you'd like to know we've averted the threatened strike. I have a few negotiations to work out later this afternoon but we seem to have sorted it all out once and for all."

"Yes, I know." Keira's brain was spinning tantalisingly around a number of far more erotic reasons for his presence. "Daniel told me."

"Daniel!" he repeated in surprise. "Daniel?" His tone

had sharpened, edged with suppressed anger, and alarmed at his tone Keira swung back to face him. Their eyes locked. He'd pushed himself away from the support of the breakfast bar and Keira's complete nervous system tensed, poised for flight.

"Yes." Keira's throat dried on the word. "Daniel called in just—" she started to explain but Eden broke in on her and her hand went uneasily to the base of her throat.

"Daniel was here?"

"Yes, he—"

"He was here in the middle of the night?" he barked at her, and Keira drew herself together as his meaning became abundantly clear.

"Yes. No!"

"Either he was or he wasn't," Eden said sarcastically and Keira's anger rose at his mocking tone.

Recklessly she took the two steps towards him that put her up against the breakfast bar that separated them.

"If you'd let me finish a sentence I'd explain—" she began again, holding up her hand when he opened his mouth to interrupt her again. "Will you be quiet for just a moment. For heaven's sake, there's no need to rehash all that leave-my-nephew-alone rubbish. Believe me, Daniel's honour was perfectly safe from me. He spent the night with Cat's family and called in to tell me about the averted strike a few minutes before you arrived."

Eden's hooded gaze held hers.

"In fact you just missed him." Keira angrily brushed her hair back from her face. "Now—" she strode around the breakfast bar and turned to look pointedly at Eden and then at the door "—I've had a late night and I'm too tired for all this."

He regarded her enigmatically and then gave a soft, bitter laugh. "Tired," he repeated throatily, and Keira's gaze snapped back to him in sudden apprehension. "That makes two of us. I pretty well came straight here as soon as I could get away from the meeting,'' he added in that same low, inciting tone. ''But, quite frankly, right now I couldn't give a damn if the whole country went on strike.''

He took two measured steps towards her and she tensed, but willed herself to hold her ground.

''And I'm not sure the outcome of the meeting was even the reason why I came. More of an excuse.'' His deep blue eyes burned into hers, fanned that ever-glowing ember of purely physical desire, and Keira gave a negating shake of her head.

''I... We... You should go, Eden,'' she said through dry lips that trembled in fear, fear of the depth of longing that rose in her to beg him to stay.

He ran one hand along the line of his jaw and his mouth twisted self-derisively. ''I should do a lot of things.''

His gaze never wavered as he moved forward again, and Keira retreated until her back came up against the wall. She swallowed, but her throat was paralysed and she had to tear her eyes from his in a valiant effort to shield the wanting she knew raged so blatantly in their smoky depths.

One strong hand came up to touch her cheek gently, moved to settle for long, sensuous seconds on the curve of her lips before continuing down to rest lightly on the base of her throat where her pulse raced wildly. And he rested his other elbow on the wall beside her head as his mouth hovered tortuously above her.

The cold timber wall seemed to chill her through the thickness of her nightshirt and robe as he lowered his body until it was a tantalising hair's breadth from hers.

And her own body was betraying her, every nerve tingling, each muscle tensing, straining to close that minute but measureless chasm between them. That she wanted to yield, to mould herself to him, was a battle she was having to fight with all the willpower she possessed.

She knew she had to repel him and do it quickly because

she was rapidly losing the skirmish with each passing second.

"Let me go!" she got out through her tensed jaw, but of course he gave no sign he'd heard her words, let alone obeyed her demand.

She made to push her hands against the hard wall of his chest but his strong hands clasped hers, held her arms above her head, leaving her body vulnerable to the still hovering hardness of his.

Keira desperately changed her tactics, turning on him the anger she felt at herself for her own weakness, lifting her chin to confront him. "This must give you great satisfaction, knowing you have to overcome a woman with blatant superior strength," she said scathingly, and he gave a softly incredulous laugh.

"About as much satisfaction as knowing that the way I feel about you, what you do to me, takes away my strength to resist you."

"Resist me?" Keira repeated disconcertedly.

"Resist you. And that's just it, Keira. I can't."

Her mouth was suddenly parched again and she tried desperately to dampen her dry lips with her tongue tip.

His eyes, blue-black coals now in the slightly muted light, focused on the furtive movement, and he groaned deep in his throat. It was a potently primitive sound that struck an untouched chord concealed in hidden recesses way within her and it fanned a reciprocal fire.

Their eyes met, held, as they sank deeply into each other's souls. And he allowed his hard body to make the yearned-for contact with hers at last.

That charged tension that held them changed too, intensified, until Keira could almost feel the electricity in the air about them. The timbre of his hold on her shifted, their bodies seeming to melt into one as he slowly released her hands, his fingertips burning a trail of fire down her bare arms.

"You want me as much as I want you, don't you?" His deep voice vibrated through every inch of her body. "Say it, Keira."

She began to shake her head and then stopped, knowing without a doubt that the transparent expression in her eyes was betraying her. "Yes," she heard herself say honestly.

CHAPTER TEN

He held her fast for long seconds, then he gave a shuddering sigh and released her, his hands sliding over her shoulders to settle on her waist.

"Yes," he repeated thickly. "Oh, yes."

With infinite slowness he lowered his head and softly kissed one corner of her mouth.

Then eons later his tongue-tip teased lingeringly across her top lip and he kissed the other corner of her mouth.

He took her full bottom lip gently between his teeth, released it, nibbled again.

Somewhere in the depths of her something began to grow, expand, until Keira thought she'd die with the desire for release. And when his lips covered hers at last a million shards of colour exploded in a starburst within her. Her arms wound themselves around his neck, her fingers sliding sensually over the silky material of his shirt, probing the play of muscles in his back.

With expert ease he untied the cord of her robe, pushed it open, his fingers splayed out now on her midriff, his thumbs resting on the beginning of the swell of her full breasts. Without Keira being conscious of their movements her own hands had slid upwards, over his broad shoulders, her fingers burying themselves in the rich thickness of his dark hair.

His lips touched her eyelids, her nose, every section of her face until her mouth burned irrepressibly for him to kiss her once more. Keira moaned, lips seeking his again. And when she found them she slid her tongue inside to taste the nectar waiting within.

As they drank deeply of each other Eden's hands moved upwards, cupping the curve of her breasts, his fingers not quite touching her throbbing nipples. When at last his palms slid over them as they strained against the soft material of her nightshirt Keira's knees almost gave out on her. She shifted her weight, moving her legs against his taut thighs, and she felt him draw a sharp breath.

"Do you know what you're doing to me?" he whispered hoarsely into her throat, and Keira's teeth teased his earlobe.

"Something like what you're doing to me, I should imagine," she said breathlessly, and he gave a soft, intimately erotic laugh.

His hands slid downwards over her rounded hips to cup her buttocks, holding her firmly against him, leaving her in no doubt of his arousal. Then he kissed her again and they strained, melted against each other, thigh to thigh, stomach to stomach, breast to breast, lips locked in heated desire.

Somehow they were in Keira's bedroom and her robe was slipping from her shoulders. His hands then lifted her nightshirt over her head. Not that she noticed that particularly. The feel of the material being pulled gently from her body was only a peripheral sensation. She was more intent on unbuttoning his shirt, luxuriating in the intoxicating texture of the fine silky hair on his chest, his hard hot skin beneath her hands.

She fumbled with his belt buckle, undid his zip, the sound rasping into the tense stillness around them. Her fingers were shaking so badly she couldn't seem to summon enough strength to remove his trousers.

"Help me," she implored unsteadily, and in one swift movement he stood naked before her.

His hands gently cupped her face and he looked into her eyes. "You're just as beautiful as I've imagined thousands of times that you would be," he said huskily, and Keira drew a shallow breath.

"You're beautiful, too," she managed, her hands sliding over the expanse of his chest, to the curve of his hips, her fingers settling in the indentation of his backbone as he slowly, excruciatingly slowly, drew her against him.

Her breasts slid against the light mat of fine dark hair on his chest and her nipples contracted, aching where they touched him, and she caught her breath as her body seemed to drown in the tide of craving desire that gripped her.

Eden pulled back the duvet and laid her on the bed, stretching his long body beside her.

Only then did Keira tense slightly as reality took over, bringing the realisation that there was no going back now. She had committed herself to their lovemaking. And she knew a moment of chilling apprehension. Would she freeze up as she always had when Dennis made love to her? But Dennis had never made her feel the way Eden did, filled her with this compelling intense impatience for physical gratification.

Her eyes rose to meet Eden's and he smiled just slightly, lifting her hand to his lips, placing a smouldering kiss in her soft palm, then slowly taking each fingertip in turn into his mouth.

His burning gaze seduced her, tempted her, pushed her momentary doubts out of her mind and replaced them with that same overwhelming hunger, that thirst for fulfilment.

They kissed again, fingers exploring each other's bodies, lingering lightly over each contour, seeking and finding each erotic place, murmuring to each other as their passion rose. When he took her nipple in his mouth Keira gasped, her head going back as she arched towards him.

His mouth slid up to the base of her throat where her pulse beat an erratic tattoo, then returned to caress her other breast, teasing her until she thought she'd go mad with wanting him.

"Eden, please," she heard someone plead in a voice raw with heightened passion, and some small part of her was shocked to recognise that voice as her own.

But he allowed her no time for recriminatory thoughts as his fingers moved downwards, intimately caressing her, setting her on fire, so that she writhed against him, crying out his name as waves of pleasure clutched her, wrapped themselves about her, rippled along every inch of her body.

Only then did he move over her, entering her, lifting her senses again until the world exploded once more.

Keira gradually floated back to earth, feeling the coolness of tears on her cheeks, and she turned to him.

"Eden?" she said softly and he kissed her forehead.

"Mmm."

"Thank you," she murmured against him as she snuggled contentedly into the curve of his arm, and she was immediately asleep.

When she awoke it was well into the morning and Eden had gone. As she struggled into a sitting position she saw that he had carefully folded her discarded clothing over the chair by her wardrobe.

Keira clutched the duvet to her nakedness, momentarily embarrassed by her memories, and then she smiled as her skin tingled at her sensual recollections. She climbed from the bed, stretched languidly and crossed to the shower, humming as she washed and dressed in faded denims and a loose sweatshirt.

In the kitchen she found her telephone notepad propped against the toaster, and written in bold black script was the message, "No. *I*, thank *you*."

Keira's mouth curved into an inane smile and only the insistent push of the cat against her legs brought her out of her reverie.

"Isn't it a wonderful day, Roger?" She beamed down at him and he strolled over to his empty food bowl and looked eloquently from it to Keira.

There was a fresh, opened tin of cat food on the bench so Eden had obviously fed the cat before he left not long ago, and Keira put her hands on her hips.

"That's not playing fair, Roger, you con artist."

Cutting his losses, the cat sprang on to one of the bar stools and nonchalantly began to clean one paw, his expression telling Keira he hadn't wanted the food anyway.

Keira laughed and picked him up, hugging him tightly, which he endured with a miaow of forbearance.

"So what did you think of our visitor this morning? A most attractive man, wouldn't you agree? I certainly hope you'll show well-bred discretion and keep this morning's events to yourself. And, since you're dying to ask, I had a wonderful time," Keira told him as he gave a wriggle and she deposited him back on the stool. "What do you think of that?"

Roger purred, yawned, and looked pointedly bored as he headed for the sofa.

"And if you say anything about a man only doing what a man has to do, then I'm going to have to say, he did it so wonderfully."

Realising what she was saying, Keira felt herself flush with embarrassment. "Remember, not a word to a soul, Roger," she added as she set about preparing a snack.

Keira spent the remainder of the day wandering around the house beginning small tasks and failing to finish them. She'd suddenly find herself pausing halfway through doing something, a smile lifting the corners of her mouth. Or she'd begin to hum a favourite tune.

By dinnertime she had irritated herself beyond endurance. Anyone would think she was a frustrated widow who had been saved by a wanton romp in the hay, she admonished herself.

A very enjoyable romp, she reminded herself, and giggled. Then she just as suddenly sobered.

In all honesty she couldn't say she had ever been

impressed with the sexual side of her marriage, and since her separation from Dennis she hadn't really missed having a physical relationship. Her career had more than compensated.

Dennis hadn't been the type to encourage any closeness of any kind during the few years of their marriage. As long as she'd been there to listen when he talked, to bolster his ego when he felt he'd been slighted, to be available when he turned to her in bed, then her life had had some semblance of calm. Only when she didn't comply had he become petulant and spiteful.

Quite early in her marriage she'd learned to pander to him simply because it was the easiest way out. And she was scarcely proud of herself for what she now felt was total spinelessness on her part. Today she would have confronted the intolerable situation.

Of course, she'd come to realise that Dennis's idea of lovemaking had been selfish at least. The books she'd begun to read in desperation in an attempt to save their crumbling marriage had opened her eyes to that much.

The basis of their problem had been Dennis's fault and not hers. There had been no emotional coming together, no tenderness between them. She'd known instinctively that she wasn't frigid, an accusation with which he had so often taunted her. Yet he had almost convinced her that her lack of response was the sole reason for their incompatibility.

No, she wasn't passionless. Eden Cassidy had more than dispelled that allegation.

Keira sighed. How different it had been this morning with Eden.

Her fingers went to her mouth, and it tingled anew at her evocative memories. She could almost feel the way his lips had teased, the way his tongue-tip had...

Resolutely Keira pushed her titillating thoughts from her mind and walked into the kitchen to prepare a snack for her dinner.

Roxie was right. There was no comparison between Dennis and Eden Cassidy. Dennis had been all show, a handsome face with no character, while Eden was all that any woman could admire. Attractive. Self-possessed. Strong in personality and body. And incredibly sexy.

Everything a woman could want. Everything a woman could fall hopelessly in love with...

Keira pulled her fanciful reflections to a dead halt. Love. She swallowed as a surge of heat raced over her skin. In love with Eden Cassidy.

"Oh, no!" she groaned softly, and the cat was instantly alert to her desperate tone.

He uncurled himself from the sofa and sprang up on to the breakfast bar to sit in front of her, gazing at her with unprecedented attention.

For once Keira forgot to reprimand him for climbing on to what was usually a restricted area, and she stroked his sleek coat.

"Tell me I couldn't be so foolish as to fall in love with Eden Cassidy, Roger," she beseeched him, and the cat blinked cryptically. "Eden Cassidy, of all people."

But what if her feelings for him were reciprocated? Her heart swelled at the thought. Perhaps his attraction to her, an attraction he hadn't denied, meant...

Just as suddenly Keira quelled the wild torrent of delight. She was allowing her imagination to be fuelled by simply wishing something were so. It was all a flight of fancy. It couldn't be anything else. Eden Cassidy had his pick of any number of beautiful women, so why would he choose someone as ordinary as Keira Strong?

"Oh, Roger. What am I going to do?" Keira asked into the cat's warm brown fur.

And she spent what remained of the evening dwelling on that very subject.

Well into the night she tossed and turned, alternately chiding herself and then sanctioning her brief loss of control.

As Roxie had said, it had been a long time since she had so much as thought about the libidinous side of her life. She was a normal healthy adult, she justified as she tried unsuccessfully to force her sybaritic reminiscences to the furthermost reaches of her mind.

She finally dozed off in the early hours of the morning only to sleep through her alarm, and for the first time in her life she was late for work.

"Heavy traffic?" Daniel asked as he followed her into her office with the morning's mail.

"Something like that," she replied, slipping off the jacket of her suit.

"Must be everyone rushing out to buy a copy of *Natural Life*."

Reluctantly Keira smiled. "We live in hope."

"No worries. It'll sell like hot cakes. Eden thinks so too."

"Oh." Keira fought to keep her expression noncommittal, when just the mention of his name made her pulse beat so erratically.

"Yes. I only saw him for a few minutes yesterday when he arrived at the apartment to change. He had an appointment with Cat's father but ended up having to leave the final negotiations to Denver. He's on his way to the States."

Keira blinked at this last piece of information. Eden hadn't said— She stopped her train of thought. There hadn't been time yesterday morning for him to tell her anything. If he had wanted to, she rebuked herself harshly.

"Megan rang," Daniel was continuing, "and he was flying straight over to join her. He said he didn't know when he'd be back."

An icy hand wrapped chilling fingers around Keira's heart and began to squeeze painfully. Eden and Megan Donnelly. How could she have forgotten again? Their relationship was supposed to be more than a business one. Even Daniel had hinted as much.

"Well, I guess I should leave you to it." Daniel's voice filtered through her anguish.

"Yes." Keira found her voice and made a show of sorting the mail until Daniel had left.

If she had needed any confirmation of her foolishness then Daniel's revelations were proof positive. Eden Cassidy didn't intend to make her a part of his life. She had been stupid even to presume that he might. His heavy workload would only allow for brief episodes like the interlude this morning.

And she had her own career to consider, hadn't she? Maintaining a career and a relationship would be like walking a tightrope.

What relationship? she asked herself mercilessly. She'd been there in his hour of need. That was all it had been.

And he'd been there to assuage her own undeniable desire, she reminded herself honestly. He'd certainly made no commitment to her. Her anger stirred at her folly, for she knew a part of her had been weaving just such romantic dreams.

The first issue of the magazine had all but sold out, far exceeding their forecast sales. But Keira could glean no joy from knowing she had excelled at combining the right ingredients to achieve such success or that it seemed she had justified Eden's faith in her.

The week had passed with painful slowness and each day she seemed to grow more and more despondent. With Roxie away on an assignment she couldn't even depend on the other girl's bright humour to cheer her up. And stubbornly she refused to admit to herself that Eden's silence was the reason for her lack of enthusiasm for anything.

Yet this morning, when Daniel had casually mentioned that Eden's flight was arriving at one o'clock, her heart had leapt in her breast before she could quell her sudden excitement.

Perhaps he would ring...? Keira mocked her optimism. She had to learn to put him out of her mind. And she valiantly tried to lose herself in the pile of paperwork on her desk.

But she clock-watched until she knew his plane had touched down. Then she set her nerves on edge waiting for the phone to ring.

Thoroughly disgusted with herself, she picked up the list of articles that were to appear in the second issue of the magazine and checked them off. Then she paused, going through the list again. One of the articles was missing.

With a grimace she headed across the floor to knock on the door to Denver Clarkson's office.

"Mrs Strong. Come in. Come in." Denver stood up and hurried around his desk to pull up a chair for her. "Make yourself comfortable. Would you like some coffee? Or maybe a cup of tea?"

"No, thank you. I'm fine." Keira sat down tentatively, wondering why she disliked Denver Clarkson. To all outward appearances he was quite innocuous but there was something about him that set Keira's teeth on edge.

Denver returned to his chair. "I've just received some up-to-date feedback on sales of the first issue of *Natural Life*, and they're exceptionally good," he said quickly, resting his elbows on his desk and clasping his hands together.

"Yes. I saw the figures too. Far better than we'd hoped," Keira replied, unable to relax, and she made herself sit back in her seat.

"However, it's early days yet and we've a long way to go. I know you realise one good issue doesn't necessarily mean a thing in today's publishing climate."

Keira nodded and opened her mouth to ask him about the missing article, but he was continuing.

"We have to keep producing the goods, so to speak. This is a big responsibility for you, my dear, your first magazine, and I know you want to succeed." He raised his sandy eyebrows and Keira had to refrain from informing him that the magazine, her original magazine, had already been a success in its own right five years ago, although admittedly the circulation had been smaller.

"Of course," she replied flatly. "I'm sure we needn't worry, Mr Clarkson. I think you'll find the second issue will be even better than the first."

Denver picked up some papers he'd set before him. "Yes. The second issue. I've just been perusing some of the proposed articles. Most of them are outstanding."

"That's what I wanted to discuss," Keira got in promptly. "One of the articles we'd planned to use seems to have been omitted."

He adjusted his glasses on his nose. "I did have a slight problem with one of them. Let me see, the piece on pollution in the state's rivers submitted by your friend, Gail Rosten."

Keira sat up in her chair. "That's the one I'm talking about and I thought it was absolutely wonderful."

Gail's passion had always been to right wrongs and she was an objective and reliable investigative reporter. Keira knew Gail had been working on that particular article for months before anyone had considered reissuing *Natural Life*, and she hadn't hesitated about including it in this month's issue.

"Did you authorise its withdrawal?" she demanded.

"Well, yes, I did. Oh, it's well written," Denver was quick to assure her. "But I thought it was just a little too provocative for our trial period. We need to step lightly in the initial stages. Maybe we could use it later."

"I would have thought we'd be far better off displaying our integrity in our inaugural issues," Keira put in. "The aim of the magazine is to inform."

"So it is. So it is. However, this article could tread on some very important and influential toes." Denver paused and gave a nervous cough. "A lot of Eden's contemporaries—well, it may not look good..."

Keira fumed at his implication and the words tumbled out before she could diplomatically rephrase them. "You mean we can't run the article for fear of offending members of Eden Cassidy's exclusive club?"

"Well, I wouldn't put it quite like that."

"What you're saying is we can go so far and no further," Keira finished for him, throwing discretion to the wind, and Denver sat back and smiled.

"I see no problem with that."

"I'm afraid I do," Keira stood up as the smile faded from Denver Clarkson's face. "I'm not sure what you've been told, but when I accepted this position I did so on the condition that I had editorial independence. That doesn't mean my decisions on the content of the magazine can be vetoed."

"I think you're over-reacting. Life is unfortunately made up of compromises. I'm simply trying to point out some small pitfalls you may, in your inexperience, be unaware of, Mrs Strong."

"Pitfalls? Meaning don't antagonise anyone considered to be above scrutiny? That's censorship. And apart from that I would have thought it was common courtesy for you to come and discuss it with us."

"And so I intended to do, Mrs Strong. But you pre-empted me," he said appeasingly.

"Your orders to have this, or any other article for that matter, dropped from the magazine were high-handed in the extreme and entirely without justification." Keira persisted.

"You may not be aware that one of the companies referred to in that article buys a considerable amount of advertising in our publications. And not just in *Natural Life*," he added self-importantly.

"No company was mentioned by name," Keira told him

tersely. "If there are any complaints it will be because someone has a guilty conscience."

"I still feel the article is too inflammatory."

"The subject matter dictates that it should be provocative. It's designed to make the readers aware and perhaps encourage them to demand action."

"Mrs Strong," Denver appealed with his hands held palms upwards. "You're new to this and, if you'll forgive me saying so, just a little naïve. There are some matters better left to those of us who have more experience."

Keira drew a deeply steadying breath at his condescending tone. "I followed regulations. The article has already been passed by the legal eagles."

"Yes. Well, I feel I must pull rank here." Denver smiled with feigned obsequiousness and Keira turned angrily on her heel.

"Then I think I'll have to take this one step higher and consult Mr Cassidy about this personally."

Denver stood up and hurried around his desk. "Now, don't you think you're being a trifle hasty? I don't think you need to bother Eden with this, Mrs Strong. And it may not be advisable to, shall we say, pester him just yet."

"Just yet?" Keira stopped and turned back to him, her eyebrows raised. "What exactly do you mean?"

He shrugged. "As I said before, one good issue doesn't mean the magazine is out of the wood. And even though you may feel Eden has made you his—" Denver paused "—protégée…"

A dull flush coloured Keira's cheeks as her anger surged. "Look, Mr Clarkson, I'm getting more than a little tired of defending my integrity. There is nothing professionally untoward between Eden Cassidy and myself," she said between clenched teeth, and he rushed to reassure her.

"No, of course there isn't. But there have been certain rumours…" He let the word hang momentarily. "I don't think it would be sensible to bother Eden with this. If you go running to him, especially at this early stage, well, people may be inclined to talk.''

Keira's stormy grey eyes held his. "People, it appears, are going to talk anyway," she said cynically as she left him.

Keira returned to her office to regather her composure, but her anger at Denver refused to abate. His actions meant she was caught between a rock and a hard place. She knew her staff would expect her to deal with Denver's unwarranted interference. But her only option was, for her, even more unacceptable. She would have to face Eden Cassidy.

Unless Eden had instructed Denver Clarkson to keep close tabs on her. Perhaps he was just covering his bets.

She frowned. Would Eden have done that? Keira wondered. He'd given her the job supposedly on her merits, but if he was unsure of her ability to perform he might have instructed Denver to keep an eye on her. Keira's anger simmered again, stretching to encompass Eden with Denver Clarkson.

Well, she'd simply have to find out, wouldn't she? she told herself firmly as she collected a copy of Gail's by-line for reference. With that clutched in her hand she marched across towards the bank of lifts before she allowed herself time to think about what she was doing.

And she was left without the chance to change her mind, for the lift arrived immediately and she strode resolutely into the cubicle. The doors silently imprisoned her and in seconds she was stepping out into the wide expanse that was the plushly carpeted reception area of the head office of Cassidy-Ford Publishing.

Behind a polished wooden desk sat a perfectly groomed woman who looked up from her computer terminal as Keira approached.

The woman smiled a welcome. "May I help you?"

"I'd like to see Mr Cassidy," Keira stated brusquely, her

still-smouldering anger causing her to dispense with the pleasantries.

The woman slid graciously to her feet, her smile barely flickering. "May I ask if you have an appointment?" she asked with placating ease.

That this efficient woman would know exactly who had an appointment with her boss and who didn't Keira knew all too well, and the competent conciliation perversely fuelled her ire.

"No. I don't." Keira forced herself to be civil. "But it's extremely important that I see him at once."

"I'm afraid Mr Cassidy is rather busy right now. Perhaps if you'd like to ring through on Monday morning and make an appointment I'm sure he'll be able to fit you in."

"I'd prefer to see him right now. If you wouldn't mind telling him I'm here."

"As he's not long arrived from the airport—"

"I know his flight was due in at one o'clock," Keira cut in. "He's had four hours to get back into the swing of things," she added caustically.

"Mr Cassidy's plane was delayed," the receptionist said with just a trace of matching sarcasm. "He's only just arrived at the office."

Keira sighed heavily, knowing she was behaving badly. It wasn't like her to take out her annoyance on a fellow employee. "Look, I'm sorry I've been giving you a hard time. Could you just tell Mr Cassidy that I'm here, that Keira Strong would like to see him?"

The woman hesitated and Keira wondered if she had imagined the slight change of expression on the receptionist's face when she mentioned her name.

"Mrs Strong. Well, if you'll just wait a moment I'll see what I can do." With that she crossed the room and disappeared down a wide hallway to the left, leaving Keira to fidget by the desk.

No, she hadn't imagined the woman's change of manner

when she learned who Keira was. It would seem the rumours had even reached the upper echelons of management, Keira reflected in exasperation.

Had Eden mentioned...? No. Why would he? Unless he'd given strict instructions that Keira specifically was not to be granted an audience. If that was the case she'd placed the receptionist in an untenable position and she'd certainly set herself up to be highly embarrassed.

You're becoming paranoid, she told herself, realising that some of her anger had been channelled away.

This wasn't a personal visit, she reminded herself. It was strictly business and she had a valid reason to consult Eden Cassidy on a matter that was of serious importance to her, a matter related to the magazine. Although technically her supervisor, Denver Clarkson had no right to cancel her decision without consulting Keira and her editorial panel.

''Mrs Strong.'' Eden's receptionist interrupted her train of thought and Keira turned to face her. The woman moved back behind her desk. ''Mr Cassidy will see you now. If you'd just like to take the second door on the right along the corridor.''

''Thank you.'' Keira murmured as she walked in the direction the woman had indicated.

Taking a deep, steadying breath Keira knocked and opened the door.

The office was more than spacious and decorated in muted greys. Vertical blinds covered the huge picture windows without concealing the panoramic views of the city and harbour. A large highly polished desk dominated the room and a matching leather couch and easy-chairs added a pleasing touch.

However, as she stepped into the office Keira gave its décor and outlook only a cursory glance. Now that she was to come face to face with Eden again her emotions were undergoing a radical change. Anger was giving way to anticipation and outrage to a far more potent sensation. This had definitely been a mistake...

An unobtrusive door off to the left opened and before Keira could move he was in the room with her. And her nervous system came alive.

CHAPTER ELEVEN

HE had obviously just showered, for his dark hair was still damp, the ends curling where they settled on the back of his neck, and he was wiping the remnants of a tangy shaving cream from his face with a thick white towel.

His gaze met hers and he stopped, whatever he read in her face causing a sudden shift in his expression. And Keira sensed his primary emotion was now a watchful wariness. Throwing the towel on to a nearby chair, he began slowly to button his shirt.

Keira's dry lips parted slightly and her heart twisted in her breast. If she hadn't been sure of her feelings for him before then she most certainly was now. A surge of diverse sensations rose in her, a heady mixture of erotic desire, pure adoring longing and a burning need to beg for forever.

Her own eyes furtively drank in his tall attractiveness, the simple movements of his strong hands tucking his fresh shirt into the waistband of his trousers. As he rebuckled his belt, part of her noted disconcertedly the faint lines of fatigue on his clean-shaven face.

Keira swallowed convulsively. She knew she was in danger of allowing his indisputable magnetism to mollify her, to depreciate her disappointment at his cavalier behaviour since that morning less than a week ago. She had to remind herself he hadn't even bothered to telephone her, and with no little effort she forced her personal feelings aside. This was business and she had to concentrate on the reason why she had sought an interview with him.

Keira held up the paper in her hand. "Denver Clarkson has pulled an article that was due to appear in the second issue of *Natural Living*," she stated levelly before he could speak.

"I know. Denver called me a few minutes ago to inform me of his concern," he told her as he moved forward to lean with his hips against his desk, and Keira bristled.

Then Denver had lost no time, she reflected. He had ensured he'd put his side of the story to his boss before Keira arrived. She lifted her chin. "I don't feel it's Denver Clarkson's place to interfere in the contents of the magazine."

Eden shrugged. "Perhaps we could compromise here. Denver tells me the article could run with a couple of minor changes."

"Minor changes?" Keira reiterated indignantly. "Denver's changes would mean we'd end up with a wishy-washy generalisation with no bite to it. The whole thing is ridiculous."

"Why are you going to bat for this particular column?" Eden asked her reasonably, and Keira paced across the floor, needing another outlet for her anger.

"You must see that it's not the article *per se*. I feel my position as editor has been undermined, I was promised complete editorial independence but it seems when it comes down to the wire that doesn't mean all that much."

"I haven't had a chance to read it yet, but would it hurt to tone down the piece?" he suggested. "Then we'll sort out the rest of it—"

"Don't humour me, Eden. If you've set Denver up as my watchdog then at least have the decency to tell me he's just that."

"Of course he's nothing of the kind. I don't work that way."

"Then Denver has exceeded his authority. We wouldn't try to tell him how to run his section."

''Point taken,'' he conceded. ''However Denver has had years of experience so you in turn must see he'd have some idea of what line our publications take.''

Keira regarded him steadily, her arms folded across her chest, the article clutched to her. ''Meaning I wouldn't. And that my years of experience count for nothing.''

''You're putting words into my mouth.''

''I really don't see that would be worth the trouble,'' she said, raising her chin disdainfully. ''Whatever you say doesn't seem to mean all that much. I thought you had faith in my ability when you gave me this job, but it appears I was wrong. Or maybe you handle all the smooth talk and leave the dirty work to your lackeys.''

''I certainly don't allow my lackeys to tell me how to run my business,'' he retorted curtly. ''Make no mistake about it, Keira, I own this magazine.''

''But you don't own me,'' she threw angrily back at him, but before he could comment his phone rang.

With a frown of intense exasperation Eden twisted around and snatched up the receiver. ''I said no calls, Julie,'' he snapped, and then his expression changed. ''Of course. Put her through.'' He listened for a moment and then his face broke into a delighted smile. ''Megan, that's fantastic.''

Keira stiffened, her arms falling to her sides.

''Couldn't be better news.'' His charismatic smile widened and a knot of pain formed inside Keira and began to expand.

''Right. I'll be back in the States on Monday. Bye till then.'' He replaced the receiver and turned back to Keira, his smile still lingering on his face.

Her pain erupted and added fuel to her already smouldering anger.

''It seems to me that this all comes down to money,'' she took up where they'd left off, and his smile faded. ''This article might possibly offend one of our well-known, high-profile national companies and therefore we can't upset such influence, they hold the assets and that gives them power. Well, money doesn't make them any less guilty in my book.''

"What's this really about, Keira?" he asked wearily, and she quelled a sliver of remorse that he was most probably suffering from jet-lag.

"It's about allowing wealth to censor our subject matter.''

Eden pushed himself to his feet. "Cassidy-Ford would never tolerate that kind of blackmail and I'm sure you know that. As I said, I haven't read the column in question but I can't see Denver bowing to such extortion no matter how covert. He knows our policies too. There has to be some other basis for his objections against running the story.''

For some reason his championing of Denver Clarkson twisted a knife inside her. Part of her told her she was being unreasonable but another part of her only saw it as a further distancing of himself from her.

"Denver gave me to believe this article would upset some close friends of yours. Some rich and influential friends,'' she finished emphatically.

"You must have misunderstood." Eden frowned. "I find it hard to believe Denver would depart so radically from what he knows to be rigid company policy.''

"Well, he did. And apart from that, how can you make a ruling on something when you admit you haven't taken the time to read it?" she asked, waving the paper in the air, knowing she was behaving even more irrationally but unable to restrain her reckless tongue. "And the article has been checked through the legal department, in case you may want to enquire about whether or not I've followed the proper procedures.''

"Keira—" he interrupted irritably, but she rushed on, anger dissipating her discretion.

"You've apparently made up your mind on a word-of-mouth account and it seems to me that makes you more

dangerous than I thought. A media magnate who miscon-
strues situations, who takes a glance at something and reports it incorrectly.''

In two strides he was mere millimetres from her and she
had to lift her chin to hold his now angry gaze.

''What situations are we talking about?'' he asked por-
tentously, and Keira swallowed, her resolve faltering under
his challenging scrutiny.

''You know what I'm talking about.'' She was playing
for time and they both knew it. How she wished she could
rewind this scene like a video movie and edit her dialogue.
But it was too late.

''Oh, no, Keira. You can't expect it to be that easy.'' His
cool smile went nowhere near his eyes. ''You've opened
this can of worms. Don't expect me to let you replace the
lid without explaining your blatantly provocative accusation.''

Keira knew she'd painted herself into the proverbial corner so she valiantly gathered her composure and prepared
to brazen her way out of it. She knew he had no intention
of allowing her to back off. And a secret part of her didn't
want him to.

''I simply meant you seem to make a habit of misinter-
preting certain incidents and I feel you're running true to
form with this one.''

''Which particular incidents are we discussing and just
how have I misinterpreted them?''

''Well, the first time you met me you had me in bed with
your nephew. You made that assumption without a shred of
evidence,'' Keira threw at him and the cool smile returned.

''Only the fact that as I drove up to the house I saw you
locked in Daniel's arms on the bedroom balcony. Anyone
might have been excused for thinking you and Daniel were
more than nodding acquaintances,'' he said mockingly.

''Daniel had given me a teasing brotherly peck. We were
scarcely locked in each other's arms.''

Eden sighed. "Perhaps we should agree that at the time we saw that particular incident from different perspectives."

"Let's wave it aside by all means," Keira said indignantly. "However, I simply don't care to be branded as some scarlet matron who devours toy-boys."

"Now that scenario you've definitely miscast. By no stretch of the imagination would I describe you as a matron, scarlet or otherwise." His lips twitched and, with a glimmer of suspicion, Keira thought she saw an amused sparkle in his eyes before his lids fell to shield his expression.

The tone of his voice had changed too, had become evocatively low, and for tantalising seconds Keira felt her conviction teetering on very shaky ground. If she let herself take that so small step forward...

Her heart trembled, parading a dizzyingly vivid picture of the two of them together in her bedroom, while her head reminded her that he was convinced he could use his infamous charm to distract, to appease her.

She tensed, each nerve-ending so aware of the charged atmosphere that surrounded them. Just that one small step, she tortured herself, and she'd be in his arms again. And wasn't that where she wanted to be?

She saw his lips move and her brain began slowly to decipher the words, unravel the message.

"I missed you."

Had he voiced those inciting words? Yes! Yes! He'd said he missed her. As she'd missed him.

Oh, yes? a part of her gibed brutally. He missed you so much he left without a word. And if his telephone conversation was any indication, he was leaving again. To rejoin Megan Donnelly.

Keira's entire body went numb. She wasn't going to allow him to pick her up and put her down at his whim. She might have to deal with him on a business level, but on a personal level, well, she'd close and lock that door with a final decisiveness.

Her lips tightened and she stepped around him, placing Gail's article on his desk. "I think you should read that and then perhaps you'll see your way clear to overriding Denver's decision. And perhaps in future Denver might be encouraged to discuss any problems he has with our decisions with the editorial panel."

Eden's dark eyes roved over her to settle on the bitter twist of her lips, and she made herself start walking towards the door.

"Is this another maidenly retreat?" he asked evenly and Keira turned, her hand on the door-knob.

She raised her eyebrows coolly. "This was a business appointment, Mr Cassidy. I'd prefer to keep it as such."

"Ah! And you never mix business with pleasure, do you?" he commented mockingly.

Pleasure. The sensuous way the word flowed over her almost took her breath away but she managed to hold on to her composure, be it extremely precariously.

"I don't care what you choose to call it. However, perhaps I should clarify an awkward situation. I consider I made a huge mistake last weekend. And I'm not inclined to repeat that particular mistake." Her voice fluctuated and almost died as her throat dried. "I think it would be prudent if we put it down to a brief lapse on both our parts."

"Again?" he put in scornfully. "I think you've said all this before."

"I've already forgotten that what happened between us last weekend ever happened." She ignored his sarcasm and finished in a determined rush.

The air between them thickened again as the silence stretched for long seconds. "You have?" he asked at last, and Keira knew a surge of panic as her neatly coiled composure frayed and began to unravel.

"Of course," she replied with only volume to add credence to her assertion.

"Of course you have, Mrs Strong," he echoed with causic formality. ''And I'd forgotten you make a habit of for-getting—'' he paused ''—brief lapses.'' He held her gaze for heavy seconds before turning on his heel. ''I have a lot of work to get through so I'll say goodnight,'' he said as he walked back through the same door off to the left.

Keira stood staring at the empty space where he'd been and told herself she should be duly satisfied. She'd called the shots and he'd taken her at her word. It was all over. Just as she'd wanted.

In a daze Keira walked out of the office, along the hall-way and past the secretively curious receptionist. The lift seemed to take a year to reach the floor this time but she finally stepped into its sanctuary. And she had to grab at the handrail for support as her knees threatened to give way beneath her.

Keira's whole body felt almost unbearably heavy as she crossed to her office, thankful that everyone seemed to have left. Sinking down on to her chair, she covered her eyes with her hands. But she was too numb for the relief of tears.

What seemed like minutes later her telephone jangled and she jumped, instinctively reaching for the receiver.

''Keira?'' The curt voice had her fingers tightening until her knuckles showed white.

''Yes,'' she got out.

''The article stands as is,'' he continued without any con-versational preliminaries. ''I'll talk to Denver.''

''Thank you,'' Keira began before she realised that he had broken the connection. Slowly she replaced the receiver. So, that appeared to be that. She'd won that point. However, the victory had a disturbing hollowness to it.

It was probably all for the best, she tried to tell herself. Without a shred of conviction.

A sharp knock on the panelling outside her open door made her start as Roxie swept in.

''Did I give you a fright? Sorry. Didn't expect you'd still be on the job.'' Roxie sat on the corner of Keira's desk.

"Am I exhausted? You know, I'd forgotten how tiring these assignments are. A week away from the office seemed wonderful before I went. Now I'm pleased to get back to my desk. And talking about desks, why *are* you still at yours? Burning the midnight oil isn't a job prerequisite, you know."

Keira glanced at her watch, surprised to see it was almost six o'clock. No wonder everyone had gone home. "I was just about to head home," she fibbed as she stood up.

"And I've been dying to know, how did you like your flowers?" Roxie motioned for Keira to precede her through the open door.

"What flowers?" she asked absently, and glanced around at the other girl's exclamation of disbelief. "I haven't the faintest idea what you're talking about, Rox."

"I'm talking about the biggest bunch of red roses I've ever seen in my life that was sitting out in Reception."

"I didn't see any flowers. They must have been delivered to the wrong floor or something."

Roxie shook her head. "Card had your name on it."

Keira frowned. "When was this, Roxie? You must have been mistaken."

"Me, mistaken? I'm deeply wounded. I saw them out at Reception bright and early on Monday morning, before I left on the assignment. The flowers were definitely for you, Keira. I can assure you I've got twenty-twenty vision. The card said 'Keira Strong'." She raised her eyebrows expressively. "In very distinctive script, too, I might add."

"Distinctive...?" Keira's heartbeats did a skip and then settled. "I didn't receive any flowers," she said firmly.

Now Roxie was frowning. "There's something amiss here." She checked the time and hurried across to the nearest phone. "Meg was on the desk when I came past. We might catch her before she leaves." Roxie punched in the extension, questioned the receptionist and hung up the receiver and beamed. "She said Denver took charge of them.

He said they gave him hay fever so he was putting them in the staff-room. Didn't you see them there?''

Keira shrugged. ''I've been having my lunch at my desk all week.'' Because she'd felt so down about Eden's continued silence. But what if…?

''Come on.'' Roxie grabbed her arm and led her down the passage.

On the corner counter in the lunch-room sat a huge vase of flowers, their blossoms already fading.

''I rest my case.'' Roxie probed carefully into the greenery and held up a small white envelope. She handed it to Keira with a flourish. ''I won't say I told you so. But I will say Denver could have mentioned he'd put them in here. You know I wouldn't put it past him to do this on purpose, just to be miserable, and he's always been as thick as thieves with Dingbat Di.''

Keira only half listened to Roxie. Her fingers fumbled as she slid the card from its envelope and read the short message.

A close friend and business associate in the States has been taken seriously ill and I have to fly over there. I'm not sure when I'll be back or if I'll be able to get in touch. But I'll be thinking of you. And Sunday. Eden.

''Well, what's it say?'' Roxie probed dauntlessly.

''What?'' she replied, more than a little disconcerted, and Roxie clucked her tongue in exasperation.

''The note. Eden Cassidy.''

For a moment Keira considered refuting Roxie's conclusion but she just shook her head in dejection. A soft groan escaped her and Roxie concernedly touched her arm.

''Keira? What's the matter.''

''He says a friend in the States is ill,'' she said inconsequentially and the other girl nodded.

"That would be Kyle Ferguson," Roxie told her. "I heard Kyle and Megan had only just announced their engagement and Kyle came down with something the doctors were having trouble diagnosing. Rotten luck, wasn't it?"

Keira stared at her friend, valiantly trying to absorb the significance of Roxie's confidences. "Megan Donnelly and…?"

"Yes. Kyle's one of Eden's top men over in the States. The three of them, Eden, Kyle and Megan, have been friends for years, so I heard, and Kyle's been trying to tie Megan down for about as long."

"Where do you hear these things, Roxie?"

"This particular thing I got from Meg who's a friend of Julie, Eden's receptionist."

Keira raised her eyebrows.

"Can I help it if people tell me things? Well, most people. You're my only failure. I have to drag information from you. It's like pulling teeth." She looked meaningfully at the note Keira still clutched in her hand.

Keira reread the message, her stomach contracting in despair. What had she done? If Eden thought she'd received his note then her behaviour in his office would make him think…

"I think I've made a terrible mistake, Rox," Keira said softly.

"If it's as important as your expression tells me it is, then go and tell him so," Roxie suggested with her usual bluntness, and Keira glanced at her quickly.

"I'm not sure it's retrievable," she said almost to herself.

"But it's worth a try, don't you think?" Roxie smiled encouragingly and inclined her head in the direction of the penthouse office. "Come on, I'll walk you to the lifts for moral support."

They retraced their steps and Roxie pushed the up button, giving Keira a gentle shove forward when the doors opened.

"Good luck. And, Keira?" She turned back to face the other girl. "I'll expect to be godmother to the first."

The lift doors slid closed, concealing Keira's flushed face.

In no time she was standing in the same reception area but this time the desk was unattended. Her heartbeats hammered in her chest.

Perhaps Eden had already left? She clutched the note in her damp palm and almost walked back into the elevator. But she lifted the card and read the distinctive script again. Roxie was right. She had at least to try to make amends. And Eden did deserve an apology.

Slowly she crossed to the desk and stood indecisively. Should she simply go up to his office and knock? Her legs refused to move and she drew a steadying breath. Before she could change her mind she reached over the desk and turned the phone to face her, punching in Eden's extension.

"Eden Cassidy."

The sound of his voice almost caused the receiver to slip through Keira's fingers, and when she opened her mouth no words came. She fought the urge just to put the phone down.

"Yes?" Eden barked into the earpiece, and Keira swallowed quickly.

"Eden," she got out. "It's...it's Keira."

CHAPTER TWELVE

An oppressive silence seemed to echo along the line.

"Yes?" he repeated, a little less aggressively this time.

Taking a deep breath, Keira launched into a disjointed explanation. "I'm sorry. About the flowers. I didn't know, I mean, I didn't receive them. I've only just found them. And read your card. I thought…" Her voice wavered and finally died and the silence returned.

"I arranged for them to be delivered on Monday morning," he said carefully.

"I know. That is, I know now. They…" Keira paused, unsure whether she should implicate Denver Clarkson. "The flowers were put in the staff-room and, you see, I didn't go in there until this evening."

"And you thought I hadn't been in contact since Sunday?" he asked quietly.

"Yes. I'm sorry, I should also apologise for—" Keira swallowed again "—I'm afraid I may have over-reacted before, when I, when we were discussing the article."

"You did that," he acknowledged, his voice low, the tone sending shivers down her backbone, rendering Keira speechless again. "But in the circumstances I can appreciate how you felt."

"Thank you. For understanding. And belatedly for the flowers," Keira added quickly, shifting the receiver from one hand to the other. "The roses were beautiful."

The heavy silence hung between them again and for the

life of her Keira couldn't think of another thing to say. When she wanted to say so much.

"So," Eden finally broke the rising tension, "shall we put our last conversation behind us and start over?"

"I... Yes. I think that might be best." Keira cringed at her insipid reply. Who would blame him if he—?

Eden gave a soft chuckle. "You know, I happen to recall another conversation we had, and, incidentally, it's given me nightmares ever since." His voice was even more provocatively arousing and Keira's sensitive nerve-endings reacted accordingly. "You may remember that night of Sam's eightieth birthday party. Apart from my abject foolishness living on to haunt me, I keep thinking about something you said."

"What...? I mean, what did I say?" Keira asked, her mouth dry. Her electrified body had gone full circle and now seemed completely desensitised.

"Something about in the unlikely event that you should be overcome by a surge of uncontrollable desire you'd be sure to call me." He paused. "Remember that?"

Keira coughed nervously. "No. Yes. I mean I may have said something like...something like that. In the heat of the moment."

"I don't suppose this call could possibly fall into that category?"

She knew they were stepping on to unfamiliar ground and a tiny voice inside her demanded caution, but her heart clamoured so loudly it easily overcame her usual reticence. She loved Eden and she had to take this chance.

Keira's numbed body began to come back to life. "I rather think it might." Excitement careered about her body in a torrent of exhilaration. "However, you're slipping into bad habits again."

"Which particular ones this time?"

"Exaggerated reporting. Perhaps you need someone to edit your work."

"You think so?"

"Mmm. I do."

"Aah. I do. Ominous words, those. And if I offered you the job?"

"It would depend on the fringe benefits."

"I think we could negotiate on the fringe benefits you have in mind. In fact, fringe benefits are my speciality."

"I know."

There was another earth-stopping moment of silence. "Keira?" he said huskily. "You also said not to hold my breath waiting. I take it that holding my breath now would be reasonably safe."

"As the rock of Gibraltar."

"Stay right there. I'm coming down. And, Keira, by the time I get to you I'll be in dire need of some mouth-to-mouth resuscitation."

"I topped my class in first-aid. But there's no need to over-exert yourself. I'm right outside."

She heard his throaty chuckle as he dropped the receiver and she slowly replaced her own handpiece.

Smiling widely she crossed to the hallway but her footsteps faltered as he came out of his office. He stopped too and they stood looking into each other's eyes.

Then Eden held out his arms and Keira ran to him. They clung together, their bodies moulded as though they were one. His mouth found hers, captured her lips, and they sank into each other. When they broke apart at last they were both breathless.

Eden shook his head slightly, his eyes shining with passion. "Come inside," he said huskily. "I don't think my legs are capable of holding us up for much longer."

He led her into the office and over to the soft leather couch. Sitting down, he pulled her back into his arms so that she was lying half across his lap, and he kissed her hungrily again.

His lips teased hers, his tongue-tip tantalising with an

exquisite pleasure. Keira's breasts swelled, her heartbeats beginning to thunder in her ears, and she moaned softly.

"My God, Keira. What you do to me," he whispered thickly, and took a deep steadying breath. "Much more of this and—" he raised his eyebrows expressively "—and you know what will happen. We'll never get to talk."

"We could always talk later," Keira suggested, secretly amazed at her own audacity, and he groaned eloquently.

"Very tempting." His eyes roved over her lips to the swell of her breasts and he lifted his hand to run his fingertip gently down to the V of her blouse. "Very, very tempting. But I want to get everything straight between us."

His expression sobered and he held her gaze. "Those two words I mentioned before," he said, and Keira raised her eyebrows enquiringly.

"I do. And all that goes with them," he elaborated.

Keira flushed, her lips parting in surprise, and he let his fingertips touch them gently.

"Will you do me the honour? Marry me, Keira? Because I don't think I could settle for anything less with you."

"I... Marry you? Eden, are you sure?" she appealed to him and he smiled.

"Everyone else knows how I feel about you, Keira Strong. You told me yourself rumours have been rife. I even considered consulting Aunt Aggie." He pursed his lips in mock contemplation. "Dear Aunt Aggie. I have this problem with the sleeves of my shirts. When I'm around a certain person I tend to wear my heart all over them. But she doesn't seem to notice the stain. Signed, Frustrated Lover."

Keira bit back a chuckle and he pulled her closer.

"Am I sure? I've never been more sure of anything in my life." His blue eyes levelly held hers, his expression serious again. "What about you?"

"I'd love to. I mean, I love you." Keira gave a nervously excited laugh. "Yes, I will."

He expelled the breath he had been holding. "Thank

you," he said simply before he lowered his head to kiss her again, this time with long, slow sensuousness, and it was some time before he raised his head.

"I can scarcely believe I've got you in my arms, my love. You know, I told myself you'd come around, that I'd make you want me, but after our altercation this afternoon, I really thought I'd lost you." He shook his head. "Since the moment I met you you've had me at a disadvantage, Keira Strong. Did you know that?"

"*I've* had *you* at a disadvantage?" Keira repeated incredulously, and he nodded.

"I quite honestly didn't know how to act, what to say. I felt like a damn schoolboy."

Keira laughed softly. "It didn't show."

"Not even when we first met? No matter what I did or said, I couldn't seem to get it right. I took one look at you up there on the balcony with Daniel and I couldn't believe how incomprehensibly, blazingly angry I was. Then, later in the library, I knew."

"Knew what?" Keira asked, her fingers resting against the solid wall of his chest.

"That my life would never be the same. That without you a part of me would always be empty. I'd never experienced that before and I didn't much like the feeling. It threw me into a tailspin and made me act like a prize pain in the *derrière*."

"Now that I come to think of it, you were pretty obnoxious," Keira teased, and he stole a quick kiss.

"I couldn't help myself. I did some pretty extensive nitpicking, didn't I? Accusing you of seducing Daniel, trying to goad you, all because, as you so rightly told me, I was burningly jealous. I couldn't decide which was worse, thinking you were married to someone else or the fact that you seemed to prefer my nephew."

"And then you offered yourself in his place," Keira reminded him, and his lips twisted self-derisively.

"Yes. Well, I sank to a new low with that outrageous suggestion. I knew it, but part of me still yearned for you to take me up on my offer."

"At the time I thought you were the most arrogant man I'd ever had the misfortune to meet," Keira told him.

"I rather suspected as much. And more."

Keira fiddled with a button on his shirt. "But the most attractive," she added with a grin, and Eden grimaced.

"Had I known that, it would have saved me a lot of confusion and indecision. Uncharacteristic confusion and indecision, I might add. I tried keeping away from you but that was a dismal failure. I just kept coming back. Not that you gave me much encouragement apart from that afternoon in your office. That gave me some hope. Even if you did back off afterwards."

"My retreat was self-preservation on my part," Keira explained. "I thought I was just another challenge for you."

Eden gave a disbelieving laugh. "*Just* a challenge. You were a challenge all right, the biggest challenge of my life. And I felt that was exactly what was at stake. My whole life. I suspected I'd found the woman I wanted to share the rest of my life with so I knew how much I had to lose."

Keira sighed. "And I thought you were already involved with Megan Donnelly."

"Megan?" he repeated in surprise. "Never. Megan has been unofficially engaged to my best friend for years."

"I know that now. Roxie filled me in. But on Monday morning, not having received your flowers, when Daniel told me you'd left for the States I thought the worst. I didn't know about your friend's illness. Will he be all right?"

"He'll need to take things easy for a while but, yes, he'll be fine." Eden frowned. "You thought I'd gone straight from you to Megan?" he asked incredulously, and Keira nodded.

"And because of my suspicions about you and Megan

I'd also convinced myself you must have just wanted an affair with me.''

"My! My! What a wonderful opinion you had of me," he said with feeling.

"Well, can you blame me? Apart from Megan there was nary an edition that went out on the street that didn't feature Eden Cassidy and an attractive female."

"Oh, yes! I'd forgotten the power of the Press. Come to think of it, I've forgotten a lot of things lately. Since I met you, sometimes I've been hard pressed to recall my own name."

"I find that hard to believe."

"Believe it, Keira," he said sincerely. "And believe I don't want just a passing physical affair. I want a permanent one, an affair to last a lifetime."

"Are you sure you do? I mean, I'm just a plain, everyday garden variety—"

Eden stopped her with a quick kiss. "There's nothing plain or everyday about you."

"You did tell me yourself I wasn't in the first bloom of youth. What do you see in this boring old bag anyway?"

"Boring old bag? What a way to describe the woman I love. You are the most stimulating, spirited, intelligent, amusing, attractive, sexy—"

Keira put her fingers gently on his lips and he nibbled her fingertips. "Am I sexy?" she asked softly, and he gave a low inciting laugh.

"Beyond belief."

Keira's eyes fell from the passion in his and she felt herself flush again. "Dennis led me to believe I wasn't exactly a success at my wifely duties," she said and Eden's grimace made her smile. "In fact, I used to think I just wasn't terribly responsive."

"Hence your intriguing statement. How did you describe it? A highly over-rated activity." The corners of his mouth lifted in amusement.

"If I recall the occasion correctly I was clutching at straws to hold you at arm's length." Keira made a show of pursing her lips. "I suspected all the time I was fighting a losing battle."

"I wish you'd had the forethought to tell me," he said with feeling. "It would have saved me a lot of sleepless nights." He looked down at her. "So, can I take it that you've revised your opinion?"

"My opinion?"

"That you think it's highly over-rated."

Keira chuckled. "That's a blatant case of fishing for compliments if ever I heard one. I'll just say your rating was—" Keira paused "—phenomenal. Sensational. Not to mention spectacular."

Eden pulled a wry face. "A simple yes would have done," he said and they laughed softly.

Then Keira sobered. "But when you and I did make love I—well, there hadn't been anyone since Dennis and I was worried I wouldn't be... It had been so long." Keira shrugged eloquently.

"I've heard it said it's rather like riding a bicycle. You never forget how."

"Would that be a male joke?" Keira goaded, and he looked suitably offended.

"Perhaps a little facetious," he agreed, "but in this case not exactly sexist. The pendulum can swing both ways."

Keira glanced up at him in surprise.

"I was apprehensive, too," he told her. "I had a gut feeling I'd met the one woman I'd been searching for all my life so you were the woman I most wanted to impress. I hadn't done such a marvellous job of that out of the bedroom so I didn't want to be found wanting in bed as well. Notwithstanding Daniel's little revelation that I programme myself like a robot once a month. Once a month? He must think I'm way past my prime."

Keira tried to swallow a giggle and failed, and Eden pulled her against him.

"I hope that's not cruel laughter, my love. My fragile male ego is at stake here."

"Rubbish! I don't believe your ego was ever fragile in your life." Keira nibbled his earlobe. "Found wanting in the bedroom indeed," she repeated huskily, her warm breath making him groan softly. "I think I've already given you my assurances you were very impressive, so I think we can disregard that. Well, all except wanting and bedroom. In fact—" Keira raised her head "—I really don't think we need the bedroom either, do we?" she asked, looking challengingly into his eyes.

The world's bestselling romance series.

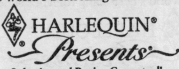

HARLEQUIN®
Presents

Seduction and Passion Guaranteed!

GREEK TYCOONS

They're the men who have everything— except a bride...

Wealth, power, charm—what else could a heart-stoppingly handsome tycoon need? In the GREEK TYCOONS miniseries you have already been introduced to some gorgeous Greek multimillionaires who are in need of wives.

Bestselling author *Jacqueline Baird* presents

THE GREEK TYCOON'S REVENGE
Harlequin Presents, #2266
Available in August

Marcus had found Eloise and he wants revenge—by making Eloise his mistress for one year!

This tycoon has met his match, and he's decided he *has* to have her...*whatever* that takes!

Pick up a Harlequin Presents® novel and you will enter a world of spine-tingling passion and provocative, tantalizing romance!

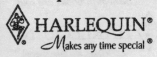

HARLEQUIN®
Makes any time special ®

Available wherever Harlequin books are sold.

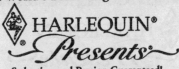

The world's bestselling romance series.

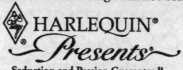

HARLEQUIN® *Presents*

Seduction and Passion Guaranteed!

SOCIETY WEDDINGS

**They're gorgeous, they're glamorous...
and they're getting married!**

Be our VIP guest at two of the most-talked-about
weddings of the decade—lavish ceremonies where the
cream of society gather to celebrate these marriages
in dazzling international settings.

Welcome to the sensuous, scandalous world
of the rich, royal and renowned!

SOCIETY WEDDINGS
Two original short stories in one volume:

Promised to the Sheikh
by *Sharon Kendrick*

The Duke's Secret Wife
by *Kate Walker*
on sale August, #2268

**Pick up a Harlequin Presents® novel and you will
enter a world of spine-tingling passion and
provocative, tantalizing romance!**

HARLEQUIN®
Makes any time special ®

*Available wherever
Harlequin books
are sold.*

Harlequin is proud to have published
more than 75 novels by

Emma Darcy

Award-
winning Australian
author **Emma Darcy** is a
unique voice in Harlequin
Presents®. Her compelling, sexy,
intensely emotional novels have
gripped the imagination of readers
around the globe, and she's sold
nearly 60 million books
worldwide.

Praise for Emma Darcy:

"Emma Darcy delivers a spicy love story...a fiery conflict
and a hot sensuality."

"Emma Darcy creates a strong emotional premise
and a sizzling sensuality."

"Emma Darcy pulls no punches."

"With exciting scenes, vibrant characters and a layered story line,
Emma Darcy dishes up a spicy reading experience."

—*Romantic Times Magazine*

**Look out for more thrilling stories by Emma Darcy,
coming soon in**

Coming
Next Month...

A special promotion from

Seduction and Passion Guaranteed!

Details to follow in September 2002
Harlequin Presents books.

Don't miss it!